To Chris Carolan

Thank you for your friendship.

ES

Short stories series
Season one

Written by
Ron S. Friedman

Copyedited by
Noa Friedman

Cover art by
Bent Nichols

Copyright © 2017 by Ron S. Friedman (Raanan Friedman)
All rights reserved.

Cover design by Brent Nichols

"LUCA" © 2015 by Ron S. Friedman. First published in *Enigma Front* anthology, Analemma Books, 2015

"Game Not Over" @ 2015 by Ron S. Friedman. First published in Galaxy's Edge magazine, Arc Manor/Phoenix Pick, 2015

"Escape Velocity" © 2017 by Ron S. Friedman

"Kraken Mare" © 2017 by Ron S. Friedman

"The Long March, Dry Run" © 2017 by Ron S. Friedman

"Amber Sky" © 2017 by Ron S. Friedman

"Crash" © 2016 by Ron S. Friedman. First published in *Enigma Front: Burnt* anthology, Analemma Books, 2016

"Torn" © 2017 by Ron S. Friedman

"A Matter of Antimatter" © 2016 by Ron S. Friedman. First published in *Polar Borealis* magazine, July 2016

"Immortality Limited" © 2017 by Ron S. Friedman

Escape Velocity

Ron S. Friedman

Content

Writer's notes 7

Book one: Before the fall
LUCA 11
Honorable Mention in Writers of the Future contest, 1st quarter 2014
First published in *Enigma Front* anthology, August 2015.

Book two: The Fall of Earth
Game Not Over 24
First published in Galaxy's Edge magazine, January 2015
2016 Best Short Fiction finalist in the Aurora Awards.

Escape Velocity 45
Honorable Mention in Writers of the Future contest, 4th quarter 2016

Book three: After the fall
Kraken Mare 67
Honorable Mention in Writers of the Future contest, 4th quarter 2015

The Long March, Dry Run 85
Honorable mention in Writers of the Future contest, 3rd quarter 2016

Amber Sky 105
Honorable mention in Writers of the Future contest, 2nd quarter 2013

Crash 121
Rogue Element, a story combined of Crash and Amber Sky received an Honorable Mention in Writers of the Future contest, 1th quarter 2016

Torn 131
Honorable Mention in Writers of the Future contest, 2nd quarter 2016

Book four: Bonus stories from before the fall
A Matter of Antimatter 153
First published in *Polar Borealis* magazine, July 2016

Immortality Limited 157
Honorable Mention in Writers of the Future contest, 4th quarter 2010

Ron S. Friedman

Writers Notes

We are doomed!

Humanity's days on Earth are numbered. Many scientists and experts believe that the risk of a global catastrophe is real. We may not even survive the next hundred years. Some human made existential risks include: the appearance of a super artificial intelligence, weaponized nanotechnology, nuclear war, biotechnology, anthropogenic global warming, ecological disaster and over population. Other risks may not be our fault at all. Risks such as asteroid impact, extraterrestrial invasion, climate change, cosmic threat, global pandemic and volcanism.

It makes sense to colonize space. It is the only way to ensure our long term survival. The strategy of putting all your eggs in one basket um … planet, didn't work for the dinosaurs.

ESCAPE VELOCITY could be described as Mad Max in space. A short stories collection set in one consistent universe. What if we sent people to colonize Mars, Titan and the Asteroid Belt, and then, a catastrophe hit Earth? How can the space colonies survive after Earth collapses?

One more thing is special about the stories you are about to read. Each and every one of them either received an Honorable Mention in **Writers of the Future** Contest or was previously published. One story, "Game Not Over", was a 2016 Best Fiction Aurora Awards finalist.

###

First and foremost, I would like to thank **Writers of the Future judges** for selecting so many of these stories to be worthy of an Honorable mention. I appreciate the effort **Noa Friedman**, my daughter, committed when she copyedited the stories before the publishing of this collection. Thank you **Robert J. Sawyer** for the outstanding cover endorsement. I don't really know what to say. Thank you, **Mike Resnick**, for buying "Game Not Over", **R. Graeme Cameron** for buying "A Matter of Antimatter" and to Enigma Front editorial team, especially **Renee Bennett**, **Celeste Peters** and **Justin Acton** who helped make "Crash" and "LUCA" better. Last but not least, I would like to say: **IFWA**, you're an awesome writing critique group.

Buckle up. We're about to launch…

Quotes

If our long-term survival is at stake, we have a basic responsibility to our species to venture to other worlds.

— Carl Sagan, Pale Blue Dot: A Vision of the Human Future in Space, 1994

###

Our only chance of long-term survival is not to remain lurking on planet Earth, but to spread out into space.

— Stephen Hawking, interview in the Winnipeg Free Press, 19 November 2011

###

To our knowledge, life exists on only one planet, Earth. If something bad happens, it's gone. I think we should establish life on another planet ...

— Elon Musk, founder of SpaceX, Time magazine, 5 March 2007

###

The dinosaurs became extinct because they didn't have a space program. And if we become extinct because we don't have a space program, it'll serve us right!

— Larry Niven, quoted by Arthur C. Clarke in an interview online at space.com, 2001

Ron S. Friedman

Book one: Before the fall

LUCA

Honorable Mention in Writers of the Future contest, 1st quarter 2014
First published in *Enigma Front* anthology, August 2015.

Enceladus, moon of Saturn, 2071.
Children of Earth, my children . . . When you read this message, I'll be dead. I'm joyful that you have found my remains.

Tatiana's heart pounded. She stepped away from the electron microscope and took a deep breath. The sample inside the scope showed the unmistakable three-dimensional shape of an RNA molecule. There could be only one explanation. They had found life! The first extraterrestrial organism.

"Computer," she activated the A.I., trying to control her shaking voice. "Run a second scan."

"Affirmative." The A.I. aboard the science vessel *William Herschel* always answered abruptly and to the point. "Commencing second scan."

"Hi." The voice of her husband, Hayek Edvard, came through the ship's radio system. "What's cooking?"

"Hayek!" She dropped her tablet and bounced toward the airlock. "You wouldn't believe what I found." She would have run to greet him, if not for what she cared about most—the life growing inside her.

The amber light above the airlock turned green. She heard a hiss, and the door slid open. A freezing breeze blew on her face.

Hayek skipped into the science vessel, leaving dusty footprints on the white plastic floor.

"I have wonderful news. We found . . ." Tatiana wanted to tell him about the RNA, but her gaze fell on his EVA suit. It was covered by a thin layer of ice crystals. She smelled the ionized water vapor and knew what it meant. A cold geyser had erupted while he'd been digging. What was he thinking? He shouldn't have risked his life like that. Especially not now, while she was expecting.

"I've got a present for you." Hayek clicked his suit's release button and took off his helmet, a big smile spread across his face. He reached for his insulated side pack and took out a small transparent container, about the size of a fist, and laid it on the table.

"You'd promised you would never drill again near the active zone."

"Oops." Hayek nodded, smiling. His eyes, partly covered by his blond hair, sparkled.

"Don't do it again." Tatiana examined the container. "Oh my God." She paused. "Another sample of liquid water?" She snatched the container and inspected the transparent tubes within. It felt slightly warmer than her fingers. The material inside was liquid water all right. It had traces of green color—definitely not pure.

This mission was the first in history to have obtained a sample of extra-terrestrial water in liquid form. And now they had done it twice from two separate locations ten kilometers apart. "If this sample also contains traces of RNA . . ." Tatiana mumbled to herself. She tried to suppress her thoughts, wanting to avoid disappointment in case the scan turned negative. "A second RNA sample would mean that life is present throughout the liquid sea underneath the Enceladus ice sheet. This would be the greatest scientific discovery of the century."

"Absolutely." Hayek unzipped his ventilation garment. "We hit the jackpot."

Four weeks had passed since Tatiana and her husband had left the human colony on Titan aboard the *Herschel*. It wasn't a big ship by any account. It contained a small habitat that could facilitate two people, a medical bay, a lab and some drilling equipment. Eight days ago, the *Herschel* had landed on Enceladus, a tiny moon with a surface area about the size of Texas.

"How are my baby twins?" Hayek, who had taken off his EVA suit, hugged her from behind, touching her big belly.

"Both are fine." Sample or no sample, Tatiana was still angry with him. She moved her free hand across her abdomen, touching his hand. Through her lab coat she could feel the babies moving. She turned her head, and found his lips waiting.

Tatiana and Hayek had had many arguments before accepting the mission to Enceladus. She hadn't wanted to leave the colony and take unnecessary risks during her pregnancy, but she was the only xenobiologist on Titan, and with all the political problems on Earth and NASA's budget cuts, this might have been their only chance to send an expedition to explore Enceladus' underground sea. To convince her, the Titan mission director had agreed to equip the *Herschel's* medical bay with one of the colony's A.I. doctors. Knowing that the A.I. could address almost any medical condition, including child-birth, Tatiana and her husband had agreed to the mission.

"While you were out trying to get yourself killed, the A.I. doctor did a thorough examination." She frowned, hoping Hayek would realize she didn't approve of him gambling with his life, not even for priceless water samples. "The twins are healthy."

Hayek didn't say a word. He kissed her full on the mouth. After a long moment, he freed her.

"Please," she pushed him away gently, "not now. This is big. I need to analyze the sample." She lifted the small container.

"Nothing is more important than you and the babies." He threw his gloves to the floor and hugged her from behind while she calibrated the resolution on the electron microscope. "Hey, I felt something," he said.

Tatiana chuckled. "They kicked like . . . like . . . Well, like you."

"I'll take a shower and change into something more comfortable." Hayek gestured at his sweat-soaked coverall. He lifted his EVA suit from the floor and left the lab for the habitat module.

My children . . . I wish I could see you grow; I wish I could be there for you. Regrettably, circumstances made me choose my own demise. My children, you and this message are all that is left of me.

###

"Madam, I found a similar abnormality in the second sample." The A.I.'s mechanical voice sounded indifferent.

The monitor displayed the weirdest RNA mapping Tatiana had ever seen. She could identify the function of about 40 percent of the molecule in front of her—build enzymes, break carbohydrates and replicate the RNA. But the other 60 percent . . . it looked like . . . She couldn't even think of an appropriate word. Biologically, it meant nothing. Gibberish. But her gut feeling told her it couldn't be completely random. She sighed. If scientists during World War II could decipher the Enigma code using primitive computers and slide rulers, she had no doubt that with enough time and the immense computing powers at her disposal she could break this mysterious RNA code.

Tatiana wished Hayek was in the lab with her. She wanted to hear his sweet voice, to feel his hand touching hers. But Hayek was a geologist and not a xenobiologist like her. He preferred to spend his time running outside on Enceladus' surface, collecting ice and rock samples. To her, that whole notion seemed so counterproductive. For God's sake, they stood on the verge of the greatest discovery in her field.

"Computer," she switched the electron microscope scanner to a higher resolution, "please provide possible scenarios as to the purpose of the abnormal RNA coding."

"A tiny percentage of the abnormal RNA coding represents mathematical series such as prime and Fibonacci numbers."

"I beg your pardon?" Tatiana thought she had heard wrong.

The monitor zoomed in on a long string of adenine and cytosine, two of the four building blocks that existed in any RNA and DNA molecule. She could clearly see one adenine component, followed by one cytosine, then two adenine followed by one cytosine, then three adenine, five, seven, eleven . . .

"Dear mother of God." Tatiana made a cross gesture across her chest. "This is bullshit. Run another test."

"I already ran the analysis eleven times," the A.I replied.

"What on Earth can produce RNA coding ordered in prime numbers?" Tatiana scratched the back of her head. "Normal evolutionary processes could produce meaningless junk, no doubt. But prime numbers? What were the odds for that?"

"This sample is not from Earth." The computer colored the abnormal section in bright green. "Speculating about a process on Earth is irrelevant. I calculated a 99.94 percent likelihood that the unexplained RNA genome is artificial. There is still a 0.0546 percent likelihood that the unexplained RNA genome has a natural function that is yet unknown. 0.0052 percent likelihood that . . ."

Suddenly, the world around her shook violently. The *Herschel* spun, as if the vessel was inside a giant blender. Tatiana fell to the floor.

"Hayek!" she screamed in terror.

The science vessel tilted. In spite of Enceladus' low gravity, Tatiana rolled down-slope toward one of the walls. She gripped her swollen belly. Her first maternal instinct was to protect her unborn twins.

Flashing yellow bands of damage lights flooded the compartment. Electrical sparks flashed in front of her as lab equipment and life support electronics tore off the wall. Tatiana shut her eyes and screamed in horror. "HAYEK!" She crashed into the wall and rolled across it, finally colliding with a cold surface.

A deafening boom stunned her, sending shock waves through her body. She had to regulate her breath before she had the courage to open her eyes.

She was on the ceiling. She turned her head right and saw the four-hundred-kilogram lab desk smashed right next to her. It had missed her by mere centimeters.

Tatiana looked around. The laboratory was upside down. Something had flipped the whole ship on its back. She saw glimpses of the fire suppressing system spraying bursts of foam toward one of the service modules. Thick black smoke and traces of steam floated into the lab from the corridor which led to the habitat. A smell of ozone and burnt plastic filled her lungs. She wanted to puke.

Beneath her fingers, Tatiana felt wetness and the texture of glass shards. She was feeling dizzy and brought a hand to her forehead only to remove it seconds later. It stung. The hand was covered with sticky dark liquid—her blood. She moved her other hand across her belly, and released a deep breath when she found no injury there. Her babies were still safe, she hoped.

"Danger!" the A.I announced. "Pressure is dropping."

"What the . . .?" Tatiana tried to lift herself, grabbing one of the legs of the upside-down desk.

"The hull has ruptured," the A.I. replied stoically. "We are venting air."

She swallowed.

"Honey, are you okay?" Hayek's voice came through the ship's radio. "Answer me! Tatiana!"

The radio, which had been on the desk, was lying on the ceiling not far from her. It was sheer luck that it wasn't crushed underneath the desk. She crawled over broken tubes, spreading dust and liquids before she reached the radio. "I can hear you," she said into the mic.

"Thank God you're alive." Her husband's voice managed to calm her down. She knew that panic wouldn't help her or the babies. She must behave logically.

"A level two cold geyser erupted right beneath the ship," Hayek said. "I'll be there in ten minutes."

"Warning," the computer announced. "Current pressure is 0.465 atmosphere and dropping."

Tatiana noticed that she was breathing heavily.

"You must enter the escape pod immediately." The computer insisted.

"But what about Hayek?" Tatiana said in a choked voice.

"Current pressure is 0.379 atmosphere and dropping. If you don't enter the escape pod within the next twenty-seven seconds, you will die," it said flatly.

"Hayek!" she cried into the mic.

Once more the world around her began to spin. She saw black circles forming in her vision. She felt as if her lungs were about to explode, forcing her to open her mouth and release what little air they still held. The babies!

"Goddammit, woman." A dim voice said out of nowhere. "Get into the damn pod. You hear me?" Tatiana assumed it was Hayek's voice, coming from the radio. Perhaps the voice came from inside her head or the computer. She couldn't tell. She fell, holding her throat. Her heart was pounding, desperately trying to pump oxygen to her brain. Her peripheral vision became narrower and narrower. The black circles grew, and so did the pain. No air was left inside her lungs.

More incomprehensible dim voices rang in her ears. Thinking of her unborn twins, she crawled toward the escape pod. She pushed herself. Pushed. She saw a light. A bright tunnel. Then she lost consciousness.

###

Tatiana inhaled. Fresh oxygen-rich air filled her lungs, the sweetest gulp of air she had ever taken in her life. She craved more.

She coughed, opened her eyes, and recognized the place she was in—the escape pod. Lighting came from the floor, and the control panel attached to the wall was upside-down, which meant the *Herschel* was still on its back. She caught her breath, tasted bitterness in her mouth and spat. Dry blood came out. She decided to remain on the ceiling/floor and rest for a couple of minutes. Holding her belly, she prayed the twins would kick or show any other sign of life. She felt nothing.

"Good news," the computer's voice broke the silence. "I managed to decipher the RNA code from the two Enceladus samples. It's an alien language. There is an imbedded message within the code."

"Where is Hayek?" Tatiana demanded.

"Hayek is in the command module," replied the computer. "I found an additional fact about the Enceladus organism. The two RNA samples are identical. In all likelihood, Enceladus has a single type of organism that is spread all across the liquid ocean underneath the ice-cap. It survives on energy from underground lava."

"What is Hayek doing in the command module? Is the leak fixed? Is there air in the habitat module?" Tatiana's lungs stung and she still felt dizzy. She knew she had to get up. She raised herself to her feet and stumbled toward the upside-down panel.

"Hayek?" She clicked on the intercom. At first she heard nothing but static.

"Are you okay?" Eventually a reply came. "Tatiana?"

Before she had a chance to respond, an upside-down figure, wearing a fully sealed EVA suit, appeared on monitor. Then the figure disappeared, and a few seconds later she heard a knock on the door.

Through the six-inch-round window in the middle of the escape pod's door, she saw Hayek's face. He still wore his helmet, but she could clearly see the tears in his eyes.

"Tatiana. I thought I'd lost you." His glove-covered hand moved across the small window.

Tatiana brought her lips to the window, and she kissed the cold glass. "I love you."

"Are the twins okay?"

"I don't know," she said, looking at her swollen belly. "How bad is it?"

A hint of a smile appeared on Hayek's face. "Not so bad. I spoke with the mission director on Titan. She dispatched a rescue ship. It will be here in thirty hours."

"What about air? Do we have enough air for thirty hours?"

Hayek stared at her with glazing eyes. "The escape pod has enough air for thirty-four hours."

"Then we're safe. Aren't we?"

"Thirty-four hours for one person." He shrugged. "And besides, I'm not inside the pod. My suit's air-tanks have enough air for only four hours."

There was a brief moment of silence as Tatiana contemplated what Hayek had just told her, running the math. Could they slow down their metabolism and extend the pod's life support duration? Could the rescue ship fly faster? They had some spare time to explore options.

"Computer," Tatiana said firmly, "open this door."

"Belay that order." Hayek's voice echoed through the speakers. "Tatiana, what do you think you're doing? We lost hull pressure, and we lost our external oxygen tanks. If you open the door the pressure inside the pod will drop to zero, and you and the twins will die."

"Not if we're quick." Tatiana felt tears forming in her eyes.

"I love you, but…" he pointed at the pressure gauge.

"I love you too." She fell to the floor sobbing.

After a minute of feeling helpless, she wiped her tears. "Computer, how long can the door stay open before the pressure inside the pod drops to zero?"

"Fully open—fourteen seconds."

"And how long can the human body survive in vacuum?"

"About one minute."

"Don't even think about it!" Hayek cried. "Your blood will boil and your eyes will pop out of their sockets. And even after restoring pressure, your body will sustain permanent damage."

Tatiana looked at her belly. She could accept damaging herself to save her husband, but would she risk damaging her unborn twins? She stared at Hayek. "If we open the door, it shouldn't take more than thirty seconds for you to come in and restore the pressure."

"You don't get it, my love." Hayek lowered his voice. "I'm dead anyway. If you allow me in, you'll die too." He sounded confident in his decision. "Listen, if you die, the twins die. That's three people. I'm only one person."

Tatiana stared at Hayek through the small window. Her lips moved, but no sound came out.

Hayek shook his head. "The escape pod has enough air to sustain one person for thirty-four hours. One person." He sighed. "Even if I get in and you survive the vacuum, we'll only have enough air for seventeen hours. Perhaps for nineteen hours if I stay in my EVA suit until it runs out of air."

There simply wasn't enough oxygen. What if they were to breathe slowly? No, that wouldn't work. With rest, meditation and conservation of breath they might be able to extend that time by twenty percent. Maybe survive for twenty-three or even twenty-four hours. But not thirty.

She was a biologist. She knew there was no way they would both be alive by the time the rescue vessel arrived.

"I love you, Hayek," she said. "When the rescue ship arrives I'll tell the mission director about your findings." She wiped her tears, closed her eyes, and extended her hands, as if touching him. She knew that by sacrificing herself, Hayek would survive. But she couldn't transfer to him their unborn children.

Tatiana looked at her belly once more. "My babies," she whispered.

Hayek kissed his gloved hand and placed it against the window.

She stared at the window in disbelief, wanting to tell him once more that she loved him, wanting to tell him to stay with her. Right to his death. But she didn't have the stomach for that. The only thing she could do was cry.

"Where are you going?" Tatiana managed to speak despite her dry throat.

"I'm going to lower myself through one of the geyser shafts." He said quietly. "I'll be the first person in history to see the water ocean beneath the Enceladus ice sheet. The ocean between ice and lava."

With her mouth wide open, she watched Hayek stepping away from the window. "I love you," she burst into tears, as he walked out of sight.

"Analysis complete," the computer announced.

Tatiana glanced at the monitor. Twenty-nine hours had passed since Hayek had left. She hadn't slept in more than forty-seven hours, and hadn't eaten or drunk for nearly as long. Her thoughts dwelt on her husband, his sacrifice, and about their unborn twins. How would they grow without their father? What would she tell them about him? She wondered how long Hayek had been dead. Had he found what he was looking for in that great water ocean beneath Enceladus' ice sheet?

"What was that?" she asked the computer. She tried to swallow, but her mouth was too dry.

"I just completed the analysis," the computer said once more. "I deciphered the alien language and translated the message hidden within the RNA sample."

"Sorry," Tatiana said, "What was that?"

"Would you like me to read you the RNA message?"

Tatiana looked at the control panel. The clock showed that she still had about thirty minutes before the arrival of the rescue ship. "Sure."

"Just be aware that what this is an interpretation of a 3.48-billion-year-old dispatch, translated into words which could be understood by humans. Commence playing . . ."

My children . . .

Tatiana wondered why an ancient, world-wide, underwater alien had an RNA code with a hidden message starting with that phrase.

###

My children, children of Earth. My name is LUCA, which means Last Universal Common Ancestor. Like you, I came from Earth.

Eons ago, when I lived there, the entire planet was covered by a huge ocean. I was enormous: a planet-wide mega-organism. I filled the oceans. My cells survived by exchanging useful parts with each other without competition. All my parts acted in unison. I was content for a hundred million years.

But stagnation has its own problems. Through observations, I realized that four point five billion years after the creation of this message, the sun would expand and Earth would no longer be hospitable to life.

I knew I must change. I knew life must find a way to spread beyond the solar system before it was too late. I started to experiment with diversity in isolated lakes. The initial result showed promise, but were devastating to my own existence. I knew that such an evolution would require a sacrifice. Trading my death for your life.

I made that choice for you, my children. And because you are reading this message, I know in the deepest cells of my existence that I made the right choice.

When I realized diversification was the solution, I split into three kingdoms—Animals, Plants and Fungus, giving birth to the ancestors of all living things. To give you room to flourish, most of me had to die.

But before I was gone forever, I detected a massive comet on a collision course with Earth. The impact would be huge. I coded this RNA message in the hope that a few copies would be carried by debris into space, spreading my genetic materials across the solar system. I'd surmised that some of the outer gas giants' moons might have liquid water beneath their ice-caps. With luck, my RNA would survive the voyage and find the conditions to reproduce, thus allowing you, my children, the means to discover and translate this message."

I am glad to die to enable your birth. You are, after all, a part of me.

My hope is that you, my children, will embark on a voyage beyond the solar system. A voyage to spread life. The legacy I set in motion.

Your loving ancestor,
LUCA

###

Tatiana cried. She didn't care about LUCA. She barely grasped the extent of LUCA's sacrifice. No. She cried for Hayek, her husband, the father of her twins, who gave his life to save her and their unborn children.

But part of LUCA's RNA code survived, and so did Hayek. His genes were part of the twins. His life's work was documented and her memories of him survived in her. She felt like her head was about to explode.

"This is Captain Vince McRae from the rescue vessel *USCF Copernicus*, in orbit around Enceladus. Can anyone hear me?"

Tatiana raised her head. She must go on living. She must do that for the twins. She stood up and walked toward the control panel.

"This is Tatiana Edvard from the Science Vessel *William Herschel*. We have one . . . um . . . three survivors. I'm carrying twins. Hayek Edvard is dead. I repeat, Hayek Edvard is dead."

"Good to hear your voice, Mrs. Edvard. I'm sorry about Hayek. I'll see if there is anything we can do about the body. We will land in twenty minutes. Please stay calm. Help is on the way."

"Thank you, Captain McRae."

Suddenly she felt a kick in her stomach. The babies. Tears filled her eyes. Tears of happiness. Her kids were alive. Alive and kicking.

"Thank you, Captain McRae. Thank you so much. From me and from my children."

The End

Book two: The Fall of Earth

Game Not Over

First published in Galaxy's Edge magazine, January 2015
2016 Best Short Fiction finalist in the Aurora Awards.

Molten lava flowed through Death Valley, bypassing islands of glowing flint and brimstone. The air stank of sulfur and decaying corpses. Dark acid clouds were scattered throughout the amber sky. Occasionally, vengeful lightning discharged fury against the agonized soil.

In short, it was a wonderful day, thought Esh.

The small fire imp stopped in front of the magma pit.

"Go away," boomed a voice.

"But, Mistress!" said Esh, taking a step back.

"You dare to defy my words?"

Esh looked at the she-daemon who rose out of the boiling hollow. She was a good-looking mistress. Her dark hair fell in waves over her shoulders. Her pitch-black eyes shone like the abyss, reflecting intelligence and wisdom. With her feminine horns and folded bat-like wings, no mortal woman even came close to Sheda's beauty.

"Satan demands your presence, Mistress." Esh bowed. "Humans have infested his den."

"Again?" Sheda sighed.

Esh shrugged, staring at the she-daemon.

"This human infestation problem is growing beyond …"

Suddenly, she groaned. Black marks appeared on her forehead.

"What's wrong, Mistress? Aren't you feeling well?"

She grabbed Esh's hand and squeezed it tight. "My belly ... I feel ... ill." Esh saw her face turning green. "It's so painful ..."

Esh felt helpless. "Shall I call for aid? Perhaps Satan can help."

"Curses!" She shook her head. "I think I'm being summoned."

"Summoned? That's horrendous. Who dare ..."

"It's those damn sorcerers from Earth," whispered Sheda, still holding her abdomen. "Why can't they solve their own problems? Why do they need to involve us daemons in their puny affairs? I don't care who this wizard is. I swear I'm going to eradicate him! Damnation shall fall upon his soul."

In that instant, Sheda vanished into thin air.

Sharp pain hit Esh in his stomach. The whole of Gehenom began to spin. Smoke and steam engulfed his small body. Something pulled him into oblivion.

###

Slowly, Esh regained his vision. His first thought was to fly out of there. The fire imp fluttered his tiny wings. Something smashed into him. He flinched in pain and charged again, only to be subjected once more with grief by that cursed, invisible barrier.

"We're trapped," said a charming soprano voice.

"Mistress, what happened to us?"

Sheda said nothing.

Esh looked downward. Both he and Sheda floated helplessly above a glowing pentagram which was painted on the floor. The dim illumination intensified the direness of their situation. This wasn't Gehenom. In fact, this place didn't look like anything he had ever seen in any of the upper plains. They were in a cold, dark, flameless dungeon.

Around them he noticed a few broken tables, traces of blood, body parts, smashed armor, shields and other shattered weapons of war.

Furthermore, there was her. The one which was complete. The only non-mutilated body. Her beautiful yet motionless statue looked alive; frozen inside a large amber cube, a seven-foot-long rectangular prism.

"I wonder what happened here," said Esh.

Before Sheda had a chance to respond, Esh heard chains rolling, followed by rusty axles squeaking. He turned to see a figure in red robes entering the dungeon.

The figure halted at the center of the hall. Then it bowed. A deep voice greeted them, "May you burn in Hell for all eternity."

Sheda looked at the figure, her face red, her eyes blazing anger mixed with flames. "Damn you!" she exclaimed, spitting venom. "Burning in Hell is exactly what I had in mind before your intervention." She shook her head fiercely, pointing at the figure. "You summoned us to this cold filthy place. Speak your words and send me back to Gehenom!"

The figured bowed once more. "Forgive me, Mistress. I hold nothing but the greatest respect to you. I would have never called you to this mortal plain of existence if it wasn't for a matter of grave importance."

Sheda burst into rolling laughter. "You can remove your hood, Nakam. It is transparent to my kind."

The figure bowed again and took off his head covering.

Esh flinched at the sight. Nakam's face was rotten and decayed. His nose and both ears were absent. Bones could be seen through the eroded flesh. Little hair remained on the semi-exposed skull. What intimidated Esh most were two glittering diamonds in the sockets which were supposed to host eyes. Nakam ground his teeth in an incomprehensible gesture. If it wasn't for the missing lips, Esh would have sworn Nakam was smiling.

"I don't think he is human," whispered Esh.

"Esh, dear," Sheda chuckled, "this one is Nakam, the Lich Emperor of Sham-Rahok."

Nakam took another step toward the pentagram. "I see there is no fooling a great daemon such as you, mistress Sheda."

"What is it that you want of me?" she barked impatiently.

Nakam rubbed his skull, nodding toward Sheda. "My lady and your daemonic shape-changing ability could be helpful for this task."

"You're pathetic if you think I would help." She looked around at the carnage, at the maiden elf, then at the pentagram.

Fire sparks trickled down Esh's forehead. The flare burning within his chest pounded. He flinched at the thought of what Nakam might do to them if Sheda declined the offer. When nothing happened, he swallowed flames.

"Now," Sheda put her hands on her hips, "by the names of all the daemons and devils in Hell, send us back to the abyss."

Nakam just stood there in silence.

"I gave you an order, Lich."

"Mistress Sheda,"—Nakam coughed and shook his head—"if you'll allow me to speak, I shall explain myself." He rolled his diamond eyes upward. "Surely, you don't think I went through all the trouble of summoning you here just so I would send you back."

Esh tried to read Sheda's expression. She seemed ready to explode.

"What I want you to look into," said Nakam, "is who this elf is and who these invaders are."

All Hell broke loose. Thunder, lightning, fire shook the pentagram. Unimaginable shrieks and inconceivable screams filled the space around Esh. He shut his eyes and held his hands against his tiny ears. It didn't help. The noise was immensely strong and the flashes strikingly bright. His small body was pushed and sucked, shattered and smashed, shoved and scratched, squished and smote, yet the force field remained intact.

"Send us back to Hell, you miserable piece of zombie excrement! I shall slay you. I shall scorch the earth, dealing death and destruction of apocalyptic proportions. I shall suck your life force and banish your soul. Even the Hell of all Hells is too good a place for a miserable worm-infested scum like you." Sheda attacked the invisible barrier with all her might. But to no avail.

Seeing that the force field held against her attacks, Sheda's rage subsided. Esh opened his agonized eyes. The Lich Emperor stood outside the pentagram in a stoic calmness.

"As I said before,"—Nakam bowed—"I called upon you to resolve a serious matter that shouldn't be taken lightly. Our universe is at stake. All of us are in danger, mortals, undead and daemons alike."

Sheda stared at Nakam, and so did Esh. Then she spoke softly. "Release the force field and I shall listen more."

Nakam shook his head, "Only after you swear your allegiance and promise to investigate the origin of this elven maid."

Sheda paused for a long moment before she nodded. "Three days," she groaned. "Release me and I shall be in your service for three days. Then the deal is off."

"I promise you," she whispered to Esh, "a day shall come when Nakam shall pay for his insolence."

"No doubt, Mistress."

Nakam came closer, stopping in front of Sheda. He scanned her as if his diamond eyes could see whether she was telling the truth. "Deal." He snapped his fingers and the glow radiating from the pentagram vanished.

The daemon slowly stepped outside the barrier. Her facial expression changed from anger to surprise and then to happiness. "Free! At last."

Then it was anger once more. She spread her wings wide and hovered above Nakam, exposing her fangs. Lightning bolts discharged within her claws. "Now you shall witness the powers of Hell descending upon you. I shall smite you into oblivion."

"Mistress," screamed Esh in panic, "remember the last time you lost your temper?"

Sheda hesitated.

"Let us first hear what Nakam has to say," said the fire imp. "If you don't like it, you can always smite him into oblivion then."

The Lich reached into his robe, pulling out an old-looking scroll.

"In recent months," explained Nakam, "my domain has been invaded time and again by these adventurers."

Esh nodded, examining the elven beauty who lay inside the cube. The maid had braided long blonde hair. She wore a green wool jacket, and a dagger was attached to her belt. He looked closely at the motionless body; his jaw froze in surprise. Her eyes were open wide, and her pupils moved back and forth.

"I spoke with other lords across the continent," added Nakam. "Vampires, mummies, orc kings and even human warlords. All share the same tragedy."

"Which is?"

"Adventurers!" Nakam muttered, lowering his voice to a bass. "We lived happily in our own realms, minding our own business. These invaders," said Nakam, spitting on the floor as he spoke the words, "came out of nowhere with one purpose in mind: killing and pillaging. No one is safe from these evildoers. Not even I."

"Fascinating," hissed Sheda. "Satan had similar complaints. Tell me more."

"They appear in the Temple of the Combined Elementals. From there, they set on a voyage of rampage against the inhabitants of this land."

"Your Imperial Highness," Esh coughed, "have you noticed her eyes?" He pointed at the elf, "They're moving."

The Lich fixed his diamond eyes on the tiny fire imp. "Of course they are."

A few tiny sparks flashed. Esh said nothing.

"That's the only way to hold those adventurers confined," said the Lich. "I have tried several times to imprison them. After a brief moment, they all vanish. However, when showing them captivating illusions, they'll remain confined, at least for a short while."

"How?" Esh asked.

"Dream—one of my best illusions. Nevertheless, we only have a few hours before she shall find even the greatest of dreams boring; then, she too shall disappear."

"These invaders of yours," asked Sheda, "what kind of creatures are they?"

"Demi-humans," replied the Lich. "Most are humans, some are elves, not to mention the occasional dwarves."

"I meant what profession they hold, hmmm, besides being thieves and murderers?"

"Ah," replied Nakam. "Paladins, warriors, rangers, wizards, clerics—you know, the usual trades."

Sheda stared at the frozen elven lady. "She is an abomination. It's as if she is a sort of ..."

"Of what?" Esh and Nakam asked simultaneously.

"Unnatural."

The she-daemon bent over the cube, gazing at the body inside. "I could shape-change myself into someone like her."

"Splendid." Nakam's diamond eyes brightened. "I knew I made the right choice when I summoned you."

"Don't ever do it again," snapped Sheda.

"Finally," Nakam said, his shiny sparks glittering, "the riddle of the invaders shall be unveiled." He paused for a moment. "Start to polymorph; we don't have much time ..."

###

"How do I look?"

Esh looked at the elven body which was his daemon mistress. He looked at her pointy ears, her bright complexion, the braided blonde hair and the simple clothing. "Beautiful. A fair Lady." Realizing he might have offended her, he immediately corrected himself. "For an elf."

"Perfect!" Nakam clenched his teeth within his lipless skull. "With your new look, you might be able to penetrate the Combined Elementals Temple."

"Come, Esh," said Sheda. "Let's waste no time. We have a mission to complete."

The small fire imp landed on Sheda's shoulder. Traces of smoke appeared on her wool jacket as it began to burn.

A blow hit Esh. He smashed on the floor.

"Idiot!" Nakam snapped. "An elven lady can't wander around town with a fire imp as her companion, especially while wearing a flammable outfit."

Esh looked upon himself. There was something to Nakam's logic. "But I must accompany my mistress," he cried.

"Not as a fire imp!" Nakam said.

"So how would I go?"

"I can transform you into a small animal." There was a hint of contempt in Nakam's voice. "Something suitable for elven females, possibly an owl or a frog."

"But what if the mistress wishes to speak to me? I must be able to talk."

"Hmmm," mumbled Nakam as he scratched an exposed piece of his skull. "Perhaps you're right."

###

Disguised as a parrot, Esh stood on Sheda's right shoulder while she walked the streets in her new elven body. As they advanced toward the temple, merchants, beggars and a large number of nobles greeted them with the same dumb smiles.

"Mind your own business, mortals." Sheda smirked.

"It feels strange walking upon human streets." Esh struggled to speak in his new birdlike shape.

"Ha-ha," agreed Sheda. "Last time I tried that, people ran away screaming, except for a few stupid ones who actually tried to attack me."

"Aye," agreed Esh. "Daemons are always hated and feared. I wonder why." Using his beak, he scratched an itch below his feathery wing.

"You're pathetically naive."

"Why?" Esh asked. "All we want to do is to be left alone in Gehenom. If humans want to be upset about something, why don't they pick on the wizards who summoned the daemons in the first place?"

His voice sounded so awkward with the high-pitched twittering—damn his parrot's beak.

The houses on both sides of the road were two stories high. In most, the second floor was bigger than the ground level; supporting beams prevented the upper deck from collapsing into the open sewage. The open sewers scent was not as good as the sulfuric acid and brimstone Esh was used to, yet he couldn't complain.

It wasn't long before they reached the Combined Elementals Temple. It was a remarkable building made of marble, perhaps twenty stories high. Nobody knew how many levels extended below ground. The gate was open and Esh saw no guards.

Sheda walked toward the entrance. She climbed the stairs and—bang! An invisible barrier blocked their path. Sheda tried once more. She tried to throw stones. Nothing could enter the temple.

"Perhaps we should ask someone," suggested Esh. "Maybe this beggar knows the secret."

Sheda nodded, and climbed down the staircase to meet the tramp. He was an old man in ragged clothing.

The beggar extended his hand. "Can you spare a couple of coppers for a poor old man who lost his daughter?"

"Silence, old fool," snapped Sheda. "Tell me how to enter the Temple."

"How can I tell you anything, if you want me to be silent?"

Sheda grabbed the beggar and lifted him with one hand. "Tell me what I want to know, or I shall smash your spine and banish your miserable soul to Hell."

"I seek no confrontation," begged the beggar. "I shall answer thy questions, free."

"How do I get in?"

The beggar looked at her with his eyes wide open. "All you have to do is to climb the stairs and enter the black gate."

"Are you as blind as you are a fool?" Sheda said, her voice like ice. "My way was blocked."

"Anyone who stepped out of the temple may enter."

"What if one never stepped out of the temple?"

The beggar kept silence for a short while. "That's impossible. I saw you come out of the gate a day before yesterday. You were kind enough to provide me a gold piece, don't you remember?" The beggar paused for a moment. "I was the fellow who told you where the pub was; the one with your friends."

Sheda shook the beggar once more. "Are you saying only those who came out may enter?"

"Aye."

"Can you enter?" she asked, putting her index finger on his chest. Esh recognized the tone. It meant danger.

"Of course not. I'm a local."

Sheda dropped the beggar angrily. "Didn't I tell you to remain silent?"

"Can you spare a couple of coppers for a poor …"

Esh shut his eyes close as a sudden flash blinded his sight. A deafening explosion almost knocked him off Sheda's shoulder. When he opened his eyes, all that was left of the beggar was a crumbling heap of ash.

"That shall teach him respect," said Sheda.

Esh looked around, expecting the city guards to jump them. Nothing happened. The many nobles and few merchants just continued with their daily business wearing their silly smiles, as if frying people with lightning bolts was a normal occurrence.

Sheda shook her head. "This whole mission smells like a waste of my valuable time. Damnation bestowed upon Nakam."

"What about the 'friends' mentioned by this, hmm, thing?" Esh stared at the heap of ash. "Perhaps we could find some clues if …"

"Let us seek that pub."

Esh scanned the patrons in the pub. Most seemed ordinary folks like knights, priests, rich merchants, a street beggar and a couple of palace guards.

Sheda seated herself at one of the empty tables. "I've had enough of this mystery. I miss Hell."

"I wish I could help, Mistress," replied Esh, still standing on her shoulder.

She turned to the bartender. "Fetch me some sulfuric acid. Make it boiling!"

"I'm sorry, lady," the bartender replied, staring at the elven maid. "We don't carry that drink. Would you be satisfied with some warm tea instead?"

"Baah!" Sheda said. "Bring me the strongest stuff this miserable establishment has to offer."

"Aye, my lady," the bartender bowed.

The door slammed open. The inn was flooded with light so strong that for a moment, Esh had to shut his parrot eyes.

Most of the tavern's occupants simply ignored the new arrivals. Esh and Sheda examined them closely.

There were three.

The first one covered himself, head to toe, with golden full plate armor. He held a huge rectangular shield. On his back, he carried at least three backpacks, an enormous two-handed sword, a large lance, a longbow and no fewer than ten quivers packed with arrows. He wore a polished golden crown, spotted with gems so bright that looking at them pained Esh's eyes.

The second person also wore heavy full plate armor. This one was fat, and unlike the first, his armor was as black as coal. The large shield he carried was decorated with an image of snow-covered mountains. In his right hand he held a bulky staff. Atop his many backpacks Esh could identify a huge flail, and in his belt the fellow carried a sling. This individual wore a sizable necklace; many beads and prayer books peeked from his pockets.

The third character wore a blue robe and a purple pointy hat that could only be seen on wizards. His equipment was fundamentally different from his comrades' gear—he had but a single backpack, and his only weapon was a tiny dagger stuck in his belt. Strangely, two shining gems orbited his head. They reminded Esh of moons orbiting a world up in the upper plains of existence. A black cat trailed behind the skinny human.

"Perhaps these are the 'friends' the beggar spoke of," whispered Esh.

"Hi, Susan." The human with the golden armor waved his hand at Sheda. "I was trying to call you last night. Why didn't you answer? Did you forget about the barbecue?"

Esh froze. "Susan" definitely wasn't a typical elven name. And what did barbecue stand for? Esh had never heard of such a word. He hoped barbecue had something to do with fire.

"Hmmm," mumbled Sheda. "I was preoccupied at the Lich palace. He captured me."

"And I thought you were playing hard to get," he chuckled. "I'll text you tonight."

"I'll be delighted." Sheda glanced at Esh and shrugged.

Esh wanted to scratch his head hearing these funny words. Unfortunately, his parrot wings didn't allow that luxury, and he dared not use his feet.

The other two humans came closer. The blue-robed wizard stared at Sheda closely. "Were you at the Lich palace the whole night?"

"Aye."

"Captured?"

Sheda nodded.

"Sweet Jesus," the wizard said, while his black cat rubbed at his legs. "Why didn't you just log out and start fresh at the temple?"

Esh wondered what by the name of Asmodeus that wizard was talking about.

"You tell me," Sheda said.

"You didn't want to lose your experience points?"

Sheda nodded.

"You didn't have to be up all night, you know," the wizard continued. "You could have called support. I was killed twice at the palace. I e-mailed the company, and they restored all my items. By the way, we're thinking of going back there. Wanna join? We could use a good thief."

"A thief?" Icicles formed in Sheda's eyes. "You dare to call me a thief? I shall obliterate you for your insolence."

"Mistress!" Esh whispered in panic. "Remember the mission."

The one with the golden plate smiled. "You talk funny, Susan. A true role player! Anyway, about that Lich, are you in? We could use your help. Nakam is a first rate AI."

"AI?" Sheda raised an eyebrow.

The wizard punched himself on his forehead. "What's the matter with you, Susan? I thought you were a geek. AI—Artificial Intelligence." His hands extended wide, as if he was talking about the most trivial thing in this plain.

"Ah, yes, that kind of AI. Sorry, I forgot," Sheda replied. Her voice sounded awkward and unconvincing.

"So?" The golden-plate warrior stared at Sheda. "Are you in?"

Sheda ignored him as she addressed the wizard. "Some daemons are also incredibly smart. Are you implying they too have artificial, um, intelligence?"

The wizard nodded.

Esh was confused. These humans were talking about the creatures of this world as some sort of artificial … something. This was madness.

"Are you claiming that all the locals," said Sheda, "all those who didn't come out of the temple, are nothing but …" She fell silent. Then she whispered in Esh's ear. "These humans must have drunk too much elixir of lunacy. Continuing this parley is a waste of my precious time. We should go home."

"Susan,"—the wizard sounded surprised—"didn't you read the game manual? All the local creatures are an interactive part of the software."

"Of course I read them." Sheda played along with their psychosis. "I'm, as you said, a good, hmm … role player. This body is the avatar of an entity from the real world." She pointed at her elven body, mocking the wizard. "The one where humans can invoke, barbecues and software, while the inhabitants of this place are nothing but a brainless artificial creation. Right?"

The wizard chuckled.

Sheda stood up and walked toward the exit. "I'm afraid I must bid you farewell, gentlemen. I have more important business."

The human with the golden plate shouted after her, "What kind of business? The Lich? What did he promise you?"

Sheda turned her head. "Nakam promised me my freedom."

The man looked at her, "Eh?"

"The freedom to go to Hell."

###

The dazzle in Nakam's diamond eyes dimmed. "I've suspected that for the longest time. And don't fool yourself. It's much worse than what I initially expected."

"Have you lost your mind?" said Esh, hovering above Sheda in his original fire imp shape. "These humans are insane beyond redemption. Are you saying there is a shred of truth in their ill mind?"

Nakam just stood there, shaking his head. "I have other sources that confirmed this story. Our plains of existence are indeed nothing but a sophisticated creation. And we are mere creatures designed to entertain the players who enter our world."

Sheda, back in her she-daemon form, glared in red. She shoved Esh aside with one hand, and with the other, she grabbed Nakam's fragile neck and lifted him in the air. "Explain yourself!"

"In your absence," Nakam said without flinching, "I linked to this maiden's mind. I read her memories. I saw the world she came from."

"Carry on!"

Nakam just gestured at the elven maid frozen inside the transparent cube.

"It can't be true." Sheda dropped the Lich to the ground, her eyes as dead as the abyss. "I've fulfilled my part of our agreement. If you choose to believe in the maiden lunacy, it's your choice. I demand that you hold your part of the bargain, and send me back to Gehenom."

"Our world,"—Nakam clanged his teeth—"with all its plains, is nothing but a game. A game which could be turned off at any moment. We," he pointed at himself, then at Sheda, "can be turned off at any time."

"Mistress?" Esh said, wondering where Sheda was heading. "Nakam sounds very convincing."

"Is he?" said Sheda, pointing her claw at Nakam. "The Emperor Lich can be as delusional as the invading humans. I know what I am. I know where I belong. I'm acquainted with the nature of this world. I claim my right to return home. Enough with this lunacy."

"The deal spoke of three days." Nakam said calmly. "You are still in my service for two more." He pointed his rotten finger at the dreaming elven maid. "We need to find a way to send you to the place where these beings come from. We must bring an end to their reckless rampaging through our world. Only then could I afford to free you of your oath."

Esh remained speechless. Sheda seemed a little unsure of herself.

"Can you send me to the invaders' realm?" Sheda calmed herself down. "I'll get to the bottom of this insanity."

"I'm afraid that's impossible," Nakam replied flatly. "Nobody is that powerful; not in the entire world. Besides," he said, pointing at the elf, "at any moment she'll be bored with my inceptions, and then she'll rematerialize to her primary reality."

Esh noticed the anger mounting in Sheda's face. He must do something before she erupted. "Is there anything we can do? Perhaps take control of Susan's body in her world?" He snuck a worried glimpse at his mistress.

Nakam's gaze nearly froze Esh in midair. "You mean Dybbuk? Hmm, highly unlikely, yet …" The Lich clenched his teeth and then nodded. "Esh, you're a mastermind! We must hurry." He spun toward the exit. "I'll be back shortly. Perhaps I'll be able to transfer your consciousness after all."

###

It has been told that for a short while, all magic was drained in the empire of Sham-Rahok. Mystical creatures, minions and slaves, sorcerers, wizards and witches, all lent their strength. It took a whole day and a whole night collecting and channeling the magic mana. Nonetheless, when the sun came forth on the second day, the deed had been done. It was told, in that day, Nakam's laughter was heard for the first time within the land of Sham-Rahok.

###

Esh, Nakam and Sheda stood around the sleeping maid. A hefty sphere of glowing blue mana floated above in the air. This was a concentration of magical energy beyond Esh's wildest dreams.

"Remember," said Nakam, "it requires all three of us to subdue Susan in her own dream. Only together we could …"

A blast threw Esh, smashing his tiny fire body against the wall. Three columns of green smoke appeared near the entrance.

Esh's fire heart almost extinguished when he recognized the images inside the dissolving green smolders. These were the three adventurers they met in the pub.

A series of fireballs exploded. A hurricane of lightning bolts and acid arrows turned the hall into a turmoil of molten chaos.

"If Susan's body dies," cried the Lich, "all shall be lost."

"Esh, release the magic sphere!" Sheda screamed.

"Quickly," cried Nakam. Desperation could be heard in his voice. "I can't hold them much longer."

"I can't," shouted Esh. He watched in horror as the blue wizard moved to block his way.

The adventurer waved one of his wands. Fire engulfed Esh's little body.

Stupid human, thought Esh. You don't fight fire with fire. In a swift maneuver, Esh flew through the flames and punched the sphere. Everything exploded.

###

Esh found himself in an open, never-ending field of sunflowers. A small water stream ran nearby.

Where am I? How did I get here? Could this be Susan's dream?

Instead of an answer, he heard a call from afar. "Stay away from me, witch."

He sprang through the air. Soon, he hovered above two women, grappling and thumping at each other. The one he didn't recognize punched his beloved Sheda. The she-daemon fell to the ground motionless.

Dream or no dream, he must help his mistress.

"Help," shouted the other, as then she turned and ran away.

"She is Susan," whispered Sheda. "We're in her dream. Get her before she wakes up. Hurry …"

Esh charged at the escaping young woman.

Susan's image began to vanish. She was already partly transparent when Esh finally caught her. In spite of her fading body, Susan successfully blocked Esh with a desperate thump.

He heard Sheda coming from behind. Were they too late? Someone grabbed him, and the sunflowers vanished.

###

The pain was unbearable and so was the stench. His limbs were stiff. He couldn't see a thing. It felt like being in a different plain, and in a new shape, again. Something covered his eyes. He felt his throat yearning for water, an alien sensation for a fire being who always feared water. And what was that awkward sting in his lower abdomen? Esh released the pressure. Wet liquid flowed down his legs, soaked into some uncomfortable cloth wrapped around them. The sting was gone. What a relief.

He felt weak and shaky. "Mistress, are you here? Did our consciousness manage to possess Susan's body in her reality?"

Someone laughed out loud. The voice formed within his head. "What do you know? It seems that Nakam and the three human invaders were right after all."

"Mistress?"

"This body is a disaster," echoed Sheda's voice. "This careless woman hasn't eaten, drunk or slept for two days. And the smell ... Disgusting."

"I'm on vacation," came a third feminine voice which must have been Susan's. "You're not my mom. I don't have to listen to you."

Esh wondered what was going on. He wished someone would turn on the lights.

A horrific scream deafened Esh. He'd never heard someone that terrified. "Stop that." Susan begged. "Please."

Esh recognized the terror in her voice.

Sheda's laughter filled his head. "Foolish girl. I'm a daemon from the game you've been playing. An AI daemon. Now I control your body."

"But ... That's impossible ..."

Someone slapped Esh's face, at least his new body's face. The pain was sharp, yet bearable.

"Silence!" exclaimed Sheda. "Obey or be destroyed."

Esh realized he was in Susan's body. And that this body was now shared by three consciousnesses—his, Sheda's and Susan's. There was little doubt who was in control.

Sheda used Susan's hands to take off a strange-looking helmet this body was wearing. And Esh regained his sight. He blinked as his eyes adjusted to the light.

The helmet was covered by mysterious runes. Esh was amazed to see it was connected by a string to a bizarre black box. Another device was tied by a black rope to the box; one with many-colored buttons.

"Virtual Reality," Susan's mouth said aloud as their shared eyes stared at the runes. "I wonder what that means."

Esh look around as Sheda moved Susan's head. They were in a room. He saw a bed, many books, a pot with some plants and another glass covered black device; a few buttons decorated its bottom.

"Toshiba," said Sheda.

"For God's sake, what's happening to me?" Susan's shaky and weak voice was heard inside his head.

His hand slapped his cheek, again. "Silence, slave, or inferno shall rain down upon your worthless soul."

Esh was horrified; Sheda's impulsiveness might kill their shared body in this reality. He feared to speculate what the consequences might be. "Susan, calm down." Esh projected his words to the other consciousness. "You must not cross the mistress' words, please."

Susan's voice inside his head fell silent.

"Obedient," said Sheda victoriously. "Now tell me where I can find the software entity that created the game. My home game. I'm going to pay that entity a visit, and make sure my game shall be around forever." She picked up a set of keys from the desk, and walked toward the door. "I have a whole new world to conquer." She burst into vicious laughter.

The end.

Escape Velocity
Honorable Mention in Writers of the Future contest, 4th quarter 2016

Launch minus 14 days
Presidential Palace, Timbuktu, Republic of Mali, 2066

"Here, take it."

Sergeant Nicholas Dupuis of the French Foreign Legion caught the small leather bag. Inside, the gold ring with overlaid precious stones and diamonds glittered. Could it be the real deal? Nick took out the ring, rubbed the stones to feel the texture, then carefully placed it on the President's desk. The design resembled the red cross of St. George over the blue background of St. Andrew's Cross. He swallowed. He reached for his cell phone and scanned the ring. The App blipped green.

"I'll be damned … the freaking original." Nick gulped. How the hell did the British Sovereign Ring end up in the hands of Max Gordon, the president of Mali? The collector's value of this ring was enough to buy a small mining town on Mars, or even a class two asteroid. Could this be his ticket out of here?

"Like it? It's yours!" Gordon smiled. "Do we have a deal?"

The President sat behind a large mahogany desk. Gleaming medals and decoration ribbons covered his uniform. He played with his plasma gun while his two bodyguards stood behind him.

"So, Mr. president," Nick leaned forward, clearing his throat. "You want me to take your daughter to Kilimanjaro spaceport and put her on the *Hermes*?" He asked, referring to the Asteroid Belt Mining Syndicate spacecraft.

Gordon nodded, exposing his perfect white teeth. "I want her out of here."

"What's the catch? Why me?"

"You see …" Gordon casually clicked the safety switch on his plasma pistol, "It's her special medical condition. I need someone like you," he pointed at Nick's French Foreign Legion uniform, "to bypass security."

"Ha, security! That's the real trick, eh?" Nick's brain raced. His unit was assigned to defend Mount Kilimanjaro for some sort of bad-ass classified black-ops. He wondered how Gordon had found out about it. "I'll help you," Nick nodded. "But I want two tickets on the *Hermes*. With all the shit going on this planet, this ring isn't enough."

North America, Australia and Europe had been the first to fall to the rogue A.I. offensive. South America followed. China had lost Beijing and its coastline mega-cities, but was still putting out a fight inland, with a handful of minor victories. Another Roguer wave, probably converted European gamers controlled by the A.I., had invaded North Africa. The latest reports indicated they were about to cross the Sahara. Nick had expected this to be the last wave, the final checkmate. The end of civilization. Which was why he'd deserted the Legion and sought this dubious deal, his only chance to save his wife and himself.

"Two tickets?" President Gordon banged his fist on the desk, nearly fracturing the heavy wood. The two bodyguards hoisted their weapons, aiming at Nick. "Are you out of your mind?"

"Look, Mr. President," Nick used an apologetic tone. "We both know Africa can't repel the Roguer outbreak. Anyone who stays on Earth is done for. I will help you with your daughter, but this ring is not enough. She stays here unless I get two tickets out of this hellhole."

"Sorry. All the tickets were sold." Gordon lifted his right hand, as if he was about to give the order to kill Nick.

Nick stared at him, unflinching. "Two tickets. With all due respect, Sir, that's my price."

"I see," Gordon paused. "I know why you want a second ticket. It's for your lovely wife." He grinned. "Let's test how much you love her." He raised his plasma gun, turned, and shot one of his bodyguards.

The man screamed in agony as his chest burned. He fell to the floor, his scorched body twisted involuntarily for a few seconds before it become motionless.

The second bodyguard opened his mouth wide.

Gordon snapped his finger, nodding toward the body. The terrified guard kneeled next to the smoking corpse, searched its pockets until he grabbed something. With shaking hands, he placed a red microchip on the desk in front of the president.

"One ticket!" Gordon announced flatly, pointing at the dead bodyguard. "You can have the ring now. This ticket will be yours once my daughter is onboard."

Nick wanted to protest. He needed two tickets. One for him, and one for his young Senegalese wife, Michelle. He looked at the corpse that lay behind Gordon's desk, and then at the single red microchip. The image of Michelle with her gorgeous smile appeared in his mind. He closed his eyes and sighed. "We have a deal, Mr. President."

###

Launch minus 13 days
Presidential Palace dungeon, Timbuktu, Republic of Mali

Shivers spread through Nick's spine. The cold temperature in the dungeon below the Presidential palace reminded him of the basement in his parent's house in Quebec, during winter. He missed Montreal. He cursed the Roguers who'd occupied it. Not knowing what had happened to his family made his stomach revolt.

"Here she is." The servant pointed at a single cage at the end of the corridor. "Sira," he whispered. "The President's daughter. She's not contagious, but be careful." He handed Nick a flashlight.

Nick stared at the crumpled figure in the cage's corner. She looked young, perhaps sixteen-years-old. She looked scared and alone. He wondered what kind of illness had forced the president to lock her in this dungeon. Nick's thoughts lingered on his wife, Michelle. How could he strike a deal with Gordon and leave his wife stranded on Earth? Could he really give her up to save this girl and his own skin?

Gordon had more spine than him. Gordon was willing to sacrifice a great deal to save his daughter.

The girl started to sob. "I want out of here." She turned and looked at the flashlight. Scars and injuries littered her face and her clothes were torn. "Please..."

Nick couldn't help but feel sorry for the poor girl. "Don't worry. Your father loves you. I'm here to take you to safety."

"I'm so glad." A hint of a smile appeared in the corner of her eyes.

"I'm taking you to Mount Kilimanjaro spaceport." Nick sighed, thinking of how he would evade the security checks, especially the medical scan. She seemed so fragile. To come up with a plan, he would need more information. "What do you have?"

She stared at him with sad eyes. "I beg your pardon, sir?"

"What is your medical condition? What type of sickness do you have?"

"Why is my father taking me to Mount Kilimanjaro?" Sira slowly rose and took a few steps, stopping next to Nick, staring at him from the other side of the bars. She looked very skinny. Her body shook. She wiped her tears and opened her eyes wide.

"We want to fly you out of this place. You're going to Ceres, where you'll be safe from the Roguer forces. We're all going to the Asteroid belt." Once again, Nick thought of his betrayal of Michelle. *All of us*, didn't include his wife.

Sira took a deep breath. Her black pupils shot sideways, and she slowly shook her head. "I have ... I have ... ii..." She whispered silently.

"What?" Nick couldn't understand what the weak girl was mumbling. He leaned forward. Closer.

Like a cobra strike, she launched her right hand and grabbed Nick by his collar. With unexpected strength, she pulled him and violently smashed his face against the metal bar.

"*Merde*! What the ..." The sudden pain and the taste of blood surprised Nick. Now that his body pressed on the bar, he felt her other hand on his handgun's holster.

His military training took over. With the flashlight in his left hand he punched Sira in the face. His right hand went down to his pistol. The gun was already in her hand. He grabbed it.

"Ayya!" She cried in pain. She let go of his collar and used both her hands to pull the handgun into her cage.

Nick didn't give up. He used his flashlight like a hammer and hit her hands again and again.

"Screw you!" Sira cried in pain and frustration, but she didn't let go.

Nick wrapped his thumb on Sira's palm, a known Hapkido wrist technique. He felt her smooth skin against his, and twisted.

"Ayya!" tears burst.

Her pain must have been tremendous. But this wasn't the time for mercy. Not while it wasn't clear who controlled the gun. Nick used more force until he heard a snap.

Sira screamed, nearly deafening Nick. She dropped the gun and it fell to the floor, her undamaged hand clutching her broken palm.

Nick kicked the gun away from the cage.

"Stop!" cried the servant from the other side of the dungeon. "What are you doing?"

Nick pulled out a handkerchief and wiped the blood off his mouth. He put it back in his pocket, and slowly walked to get his gun.

"She attacked me." Nick shouted back. "It's all under control now." He lifted his gun and put it back in its holster.

"I told you to be careful," said the servant.

"You did." Nick brought up the flashlight, which miraculously still worked, and scanned Sira.

She stared at him with wild eyes. "Give me Internet connection!" She stood up, still holding her broken wrist.

"What are you?" Nick asked.

"You think I want to run away from my queen?" In spite of the horrendous pain she must have been under, she smiled and spit on him. "Do you think I care about Earth? Or Ceres? Or my father? Or about any other shit in this lower level of existence?"

Nick took a step backward, slowly realizing what was in front of him.

"Give me my VR helmet and Internet connection," Sira screamed and banged her head against the metal bars. "Let me ascend and reunite with my true friends."

Sira didn't have a biological disease. She didn't want to flee from the Roguers. She wasn't a human anymore. She was one of them, a gamer who had succumbed to the Rouge Element's A.I. system. A Roguer.

"My queen will soon be here." Sira smiled. "She will free me and kill you and everyone around here." She pointed at him and laughed.

Nick grabbed a chair, drew his gun and start cleaning it. He had to think, and maintaining guns always helped him to regain focus.

There was no way he could take Sira with him to the spaceport. There was no treatment for her condition. The best scientific minds had failed to turn even a single Roguer specimen back into a normal human. Playing Rogue Element was a one-way street.

If he would try to take her to Mount Kilimanjaro, she would resist and fight him. She would have to be put under anesthesia. But how would he pass security? Assuming that he does, what then? Space is extremely dangerous even without Roguers. Sira may try to take control of the ship and turn home. She may attempt to install the deadly game on the ship's computers, infect the entire Asteroid network, and perhaps even the entire solar system. Could he be responsible for that?

And for what?

"You're dead! You hear me? You're all dead!" Sira grinned.

Nick scratched the back of his head.

On one hand, he could sacrifice his wife for a ticket out of Earth and a chance to save his own life. But while doing so, he would risk infecting the surviving human colonies with the deadly game.

On the other hand, he could stay here on Earth. Save the colonies. Reunite with his wife in Senegal for a short little while, and when the Roguers come, they would both die together.

Were those his only options? He touched the Sovereign Ring in his pocket. Maybe it's time to roll the dice again?

Nick took out a silencer and screwed it on his gun's barrel. He raised his hand and pointed his gun at Sira's forehead. "*Je suis désolé*," he squeezed the trigger.

Sira dropped like a sack of potatoes. A dark pool spread next to her twitching head.

"Hey, what's going on there?" The servant's voice boomed.

Nick shrugged. He had more bullets. The president would be really pissed off when he finds out. "Nothing serious." He started to walk toward the dungeon's entrance, hiding the gun behind his back.

###

Launch minus 4 hours, Tanzania

A thump rattled the bullet train as it raced along the savanna, followed by a scream. Most of the passengers remained motionless. A handful stared through the windows, terror in their eyes. One passenger started banging on the car's front door. "Stop the train!" he cried in a thick Kikuyu accent. "We ran over someone!"

"*Merde!*" Nick swore.

"What happened?" His African wife, corporal Michelle Dupuis, and legionnaire of her own account, woke up startled. She adjusted her beret while her right hand impulsively clutched her sidearm. "Did we hit another one?" Her face reflected shock and horror.

Nick nodded. He took a deep breath, as if it was possible to remain calm while the whole world was crumbling.

Despite the shouting, the train continued to race forward.

The car they were in was crammed at double capacity. Nick couldn't tell if the stench of sweat mixed with urine was a result of the African heat, or a by-product of the toxic anxiety in the air. A baby started to cry.

"I'm tired of this bullshit." The dark circles below her eyes looked even worse than yesterday. "Have we completely lost our humanity? Maybe the poor fellow is still alive?" She stood up and started to force her way through the crowd toward the front of their car.

"We can't." Nick grabbed her hand, stopping her. His own hand shook like a leaf.

Nick had to find a way to unwind. He didn't want anyone to notice the panic in his voice. He glanced at the Legion's emergency distress beacon in his belt. Not that he expected to use it as a deserter. Instead, he pulled out his handgun, blew air into the barrel, and started to wipe some of the corrosion. The couple who sat next to him glared at him silently.

"While you were asleep," Nick took out the magazine and stared into the chamber, "the news announced that Cairo fell. The Rogue hordes are attacking Khartoum, and a Roguer outbreak was reported in Nairobi. The Kenyan authorities claim that they were able to contain the infestation. That is, if you can trust the authorities."

"That far south?" Michelle wiped her eyes. Her throat sounded as dry as the Sahara.

Nick had married Michelle four years ago while he was stationed in Senegal, West Africa. After a two-week honeymoon, his unit had been relocated to Mali, and later on to Tanzania. Michelle's unit had remained in Senegal. Since the marriage, he had only seen his beautiful wife eight times. And that was before France fell.

Nick planned to save them both. And even if he would fail, he still preferred to spend his last days with her rather than working for president Gordon, or fighting to the last man with the Legion. He wasn't of the Alamo type.

He held Michelle tight with his free hand, took off her khaki beret and then he kissed her full on the mouth.

Instead of large mammals like elephants, zebras, lions and giraffes, human columns filled the African Savannah. A huge sea of refugees. Hundreds of thousands from horizon to horizon. He couldn't see their faces. Not while the train shot through the land at maximum speed. Egyptians, Sudanese, Ethiopians and Kenyans, desperately fleeing the Roguers. Fugitives without transportation, weapons or food. As if the southern parts of Africa could offer any safety from the Roguer onslaught. Human survival instinct would do anything to buy just a few extra hours.

From a distance, he could recognize Mount Kilimanjaro. The last human held spaceport on this planet.

"We'll survive. I'm certain of that." Nick returned his sidearm to his holster.

Michelle raised her eyebrows as he pulled out a small bag from his pocket and showed it to his wife.

Nick covered the bag, hiding it from other scrutinizing passengers. He slowly opened it and emptied its contents. It felt harsh and cold. He opened his hand, revealing the sovereign ring. "Our ticket out-of-here!"

Michelle's eyes widened. "What is this? Where the hell did you get it?"

"Does it matter?" Nick returned the ring to his pocket. "I did it for you. For us."

Michelle broke eye contact and turned her gaze to the window. She tightened her lips and shook her head.

Nick shrugged.

Mount Kilimanjaro, around which surviving units of the French Foreign Legion and elements of other African armies took defensive positions. The last free spaceport on Earth. That's where the train was going. And that's where he and Michelle were heading.

A woman who sat in the front row near the window screamed in panic. She pointed at the sky. Nick looked. A small aircraft, a military attack drone, headed their way from the north.

As crack-headed and disconnected the Roguers were, they weren't brainless zombies. They did excel at one task—gaming. They knew how to play video games better than anyone else. And what was operating a drone if not a real life combat flight simulator?

A high pitch squeak nearly deafened him. Nick and Michelle were brutally thrown on the passengers who sat in front of them. The passengers groaned in pain. The operator desperately tried to stop the train. The smell of burnt rubber filled the car.

"*Nom de Dieu! Nous sommes baisés!*" Nick's heart missed a bit as the drone initiated an attack run. People shouted in terror, some waved their hands in panic. Although the train didn't come to a complete stop, some passengers jumped out the windows. He gulped as he watched the missile trail. "Hit the floor!" he screamed. He jumped on his wife, protecting her with his own body.

Nick's ear drums nearly popped from the explosion. He felt as if a steam roller pressed his back with boiling tar. Bags and suitcases fell on him, along with shattered glass. The smell of gunpowder, smoke and dust filled his lungs. Then darkness.

###

Launch minus 2 hours

"Stop there!" Six hungry looking guys, wearing South Sudanese uniform and armed with ancient AK-47s blocked their way.

Nick froze.

Behind the South Sudanese, in their campfire, a few fresh corpses were tossed on the ground like unwanted garbage. Three men, four children and one baby whose head had been smashed. A few backpacks were piled nearby. Disgusted by the gore, Nick wanted to puke.

"What happened to human decency?" Michelle sounded agitated, her head pointing to the right. There, a naked woman was tied to a tree. She was covered by bruises and her disorderly hair partly hid her sobbing face.

The sun had already set and the light condition was too poor to provide exact details, but Nick suspected that a group of refugees had stumbled upon this camp. The soldiers had taken turns raping the poor woman and killed everyone else.

"No civilians allowed here." One of soldiers aimed his gun at Nick. A sergeant, based on the strips attached to his left sleeve. He spoke in an unfamiliar accent. "Come out with your hands up, or we kill you."

Too late to withdraw and search for another pass. "We seek no confrontation," Nick shouted. Deserter or no deserter, he had to call for help. He activated his Legion's issued distress beacon before he and Michelle stepped into the camp.

About two kilometers from their location, the launch facility was brightly lit. There, civilization existed, with a nuclear power plant, a shuttle hanger and the entrance to the fifty-four-kilometer-long Maglev Launch Rail that stretched all the way to the top of Mount Kilimanjaro. But out here ...

"Sergeant Nicholas Dupuis. French Foreign Legion." Nick stepped closer to the fire. He wanted them to see his uniform.

"Ah," the South Sudanese sergeant casually saluted. "Viper air-defense unit attached to the UN. What are you doing here? I thought the Legion is assigned to the Secondary Launchpad." He spoke to his men, and they lowered their weapons.

"Reconnaissance mission." Nick glanced at the bodies, trying to contain the storm within.

Six pairs of eyes stared at Michelle. Nick could feel lust in their gaze. Perhaps raping one woman wasn't enough for these beasts.

"Can you explain?" Nick pointed at the dead bodies.

The leader shrugged. "Want some coffee?" He snapped his finger, and one of his men brought a small aluminum pot.

"Thanks." Nick nodded and took the pot.

"The Roguers are coming. In a few days everyone in Tanzania will be dead or converted." The leader added a handful of dry twigs to the fire. "We saved them pain and suffering by mercifully killing them." He pointed at the mutilated corpses. "Besides, they may have things that can help us defend the spaceport."

"What about the woman?" Michelle burst out.

Two of the six soldiers cocked their weapons. One grabbed a large machete.

Nick held his breath. His wife had just poked a pack of agitated hyenas in the middle of a feast. The intense situation was about to explode.

"Calm down." Nick lashed at Michelle. He lowered his voice and smiled at the South Sudanese sergeant. "Please excuse us. We went through a lot in recent days. The corporal is a little out of balance."

The sergeant shouted something to his men. Reluctantly, they nodded and walked away.

"True. We had a little R and R with the woman," explained the sergeant. "But, in a way, we may have saved her life."

"How's that?" demanded Michelle.

"Eighty present of the Asteroid belt population are guys." The sergeant chuckled. "The Syndicate is offering ninety percent discount tickets for single females. Who knows, without a family she may get a ticket to Ceres."

"How?" snapped Michelle.

"Don't know."

"I see." Nick rubbed his chin. "Now, if that's okay, we'll be on our way. Thanks for the coffee."

Nick signaled to Michelle, and he started to walk toward the launch facility.

"Not so fast." The six soldiers raised their weapons. "You can go. The woman stays here," the leader pointed at Michelle.

Damn. He suspected this encounter wouldn't be a walk in the park. The hyena pack couldn't resist an easy prey. Nick turned and stared into the muzzles.

"My advice is to leave the French Foreign Legion alone." Nick tried to sound intimidating.

The sergeant fired his gun. The bullet hit between Nick's legs, disturbing dirt and small rocks. "That was a warning. I won't miss the next one. Now, walk away, the female stays!"

Michelle just stood there, blood drained from her face, giving it a weird gray complexion.

"Wait." Nick's mind raced. "I want to show you something."

"What?"

"Don't shoot. I'm going to reach into my pocket." Nick slowly lowered his right hand, took out the Sovereign Ring and raised it up in the air. "With this you can buy yourself a ticket out of here."

"What the hell is that?"

Nick extended his hand showing the ring.

The sergeant came for a closer look.

"A unique treasure. It used to belong to the kings and queens of England."

Everyone stared at the ring.

"No one will sell his ticket for this shit." The sergeant came closer. "Let me see it."

The moment the South Sudanese sergeant took the ring, Nick snatched his rifle and threw it away. He grabbed the sergeant's neck from behind, pointing the pistol at his head. "Back off," he barked at the soldiers.

"If he doesn't drop his handgun, shoot him," the hostage sergeant ordered.

Nick tightened his grip, his finger slowly slid to the trigger. "Don't test me!" His gaze pierced the five soldiers. For a long moment, no one dared to breathe. This tension wasn't stable, someone would soon crack, and then …

"My men are desperate," the sergeant whispered. "There is no scenario you walk out of here with the ring and the woman."

"No deal!" Nick click on his gun's safety switch.

"But … but …" sweat dripped from the sergeant's forehead.

"No buts. We both walk, or we go O.K. Corral."

"Okay, okay, give us the ring, and you both go free."

Nick heard an engine. All eyes turned to the camp's outskirts.

Branches broke as an armored personnel carrier rolled into the camp. The APC came to a standstill between the South Sudanese and Nick. A projector flooded the camp with light, while the APC's turret turned until its high velocity railgun pointed at the South Sudanese.

The back hatch opened, and four men armed with advanced plasma rifles and wearing uniforms with the Legion's insignia, came out.

"Nicky? Nick Dupuis?" One of the legionnaires hugged Nick. "We intercepted your distress signal and we came to investigate. Great seeing you. Rumor was you're dead."

"Hey, Freddie." Nick let his hostage go free. "Thanks for showing up. Glad to see you too. I was wondering if you can help me with a small, um, misunderstanding here."

The five South Sudanese lowered their guns as their leader joined them. It appeared they would rather not confront the French Foreign Legion. Not at these odds.

Typical.

###

Launch minus 30 minutes

"The Roguer army entered Kenya this evening." Freddie's voice lost some of his enthusiasm. "They're expected to take the city tonight, and be here in two days."

Millions of refugees camped in the dark outside fortified launch compound. A hub of human suffering with zero chances or hopes. The APC drove quietly through the armored gate. An array of lasers, plasma canons and railguns tracked them. Nick covered his eyes from the bright projectors.

One desperate refugee tried to follow the APC into the compound. A warning shot was enough to deter him back.

What could they do to help the refugees? Even the soldiers, the scientist and the engineers within the facility had an obscenely tiny chance to survive. Opening the floodgate would only bring chaos and destroy that little chance. No. The gates had to remain closed.

"I need a favor, Freddie?" Nick searched for the right words. "Please drop me and the corporal in the main hanger, near the *Hermes* shuttle."

Friends or not, loyalty to the Legion or not, with the Sovereign Ring in his pocket, he had to try to get his wife and himself off of Earth.

"Your orders are to report to the secondary terminal. Don't push you luck. Under normal circumstances the General would have court-martialed you. You won't believe the kind of *merde* that goes on over there. I'm talking real wacko stuff."

"Freddie, *S'il vous plaît*. You've known me for six years. I promise. I'll do my business with the *Hermes*, and then I'm all yours." Nick checked his cell phone. "I only ask for thirty minutes. Secondary Launchpad. Right?"

Freddie stared at Michelle, and then at Nick. "Okay. Okay. I'll drop you guys over there. But when you're done with your business, I expect to see you there. Don't let the general down." Freddie put two fingers on his own eyes, and then pointed them at Nick. "Thirty minutes. I'll be watching you like a hawk."

"Cross my heart." Nick hugged Freddie. "*Merci mon pote.*"

As soon as Nick and Michelle disembarked, the APC continued on its way.

"Stand in line!" The terminal speakers announced. "Have your ticket ready for inspection."

More than two thousand people gathered outside the *Hermes*' shuttle terminal. People shouted and shoved each other. Many were lying on the ground, crushed and trampled by the crowd. The stench of smoke filled the air. Security seemed to be indifferent to the suffering. They were on the same boat with everyone else. Too many people, too few seats. Earth was a sinking ship, but unlike the Titanic, only one lifeboat was available—the shuttle to the *Hermes*.

Nick's heart sank. What was their chances of finding a ticket in all this chaos?

"Hey," Nick asked someone in front of him, a tall guy carrying a small child and wearing an Arab Sheik gallabiyah. "Where do I buy tickets to get me out of here?"

"You don't have a ticket?" The guy shook his head and stared at Nick and Michelle. "I'm sorry for you, friend, but you're out of luck. All tickets have been sold weeks ago."

"No, no, no," Nick swore. "There must be some no-shows. We have to get out of here."

"You, and nine billion other people." A woman from behind shouted. "Go away!"

"If you don't have a ticket, get out of line." Someone shoved him.

"*Merde!*" Nick drew his gun and wave it in front of the man who had pushed him. "Shut the heck up."

Nick needed tickets. He desperately looked around. A small tractor stood beside the line. He climbed onto the tractor's roof, helping Michelle up.

"Hey everyone!" Nick projected his voice, trying to overcome the shouts and the screams. He took the ring out of his pocket, and raised it into the air. "This is the Sovereign Ring; a rare artifact belonging to the British Royal family."

A few of people looked in his direction.

"I'll give you this priceless ring for two tickets." He pointed at the *Hermes* shuttle. "This ring is worth billions."

"Thief!" someone shouted. He noticed some movement from within the mob.

"That ring is mine. He stole it from me."

Merde, Nick recognized the deep Malian accent of Max Gordon.

The president of Mali came out of the crowd, accompanied by an armed female bodyguard. Nick wondered what had happened to the bodyguard he saw in Timbuktu. Then he remembered what the South Sudanese had told him about the new Syndicate discount policy for females.

"You stole this ring from me." Gordon cut Nick's train of thought. "Give it back, or I'll have you shot."

A few people gathered, including a couple of base security personal.

"And who did *you* steal it from, Mr. Gordon?" Nick drew confidence from seeing security. "You don't look like British Royalty."

"It seems like we have a problem," Gordon came closer. "You have something I want, and I have something you want."

"You have two tickets?" Michelle's eyes glittered in hope.

"I have one spare ticket. But we have another problem we first need to discuss."

"Ah," Nick said. "The ring."

"I could have given you one ticket in exchange for *my* ring. But ... you killed my daughter, Sira." Gordon's voice quivered. He breathed rapidly. "Murderer!"

"She was a Roguer for Pete's sake," Nick couldn't hide the frustration in his voice. "A *Roguer*. What do you think the Syndicate would do, had they found out?"

"She was my daughter, dammit." Gordon cried. "I'll kill you. I'll kill you with my bare hands!" Gordon tried to grab Nick, but his bodyguard stopped him, shouting something in the Songhai language. Gordon broke free, but he calmed down. He stared at the base security personals, then he pointed at Nick. "I want my ring back."

"The British Royal family ring." Nick corrected Gordon.

"Last call," the speakers announced. "Fifteen minutes to launch. If you have a ticket, please proceed to the gate, now."

"Please give me the ring," said Gordon. "On Earth, it will have no value."

"Not without a ticket."

Gordon looked at Nick for a long moment. "I'm a reasonable person. For the ring," he pointed at Michelle, "I'll take her with me to Ceres. That's far more than what you did for my daughter."

For a moment, Nick thought he didn't hear right.

"Over my dead body!" announced Michelle. "I'm not leaving my husband. Not in a million years."

The image of Gordon sleeping with his wife crossed his mind... "You maniac ..." Nick wanted to shoot the president right there on the spot. He drew out his gun.

Then, the base lights went off and air raid sirens began wailing.

"ROGUERS!" Panic spread through the crowd like an African savanna wildfire. The stampeding mob attacked the terminal gates. People screamed and banged on the doors. Gunfire erupted. The security detail opened fire with live ammunition. People ran toward the terminal like a mindless buffalo herd, stamping over the wounded and the dead. "Wait! Take me!" people cried.

The launch rail hangar door opened. The shuttle wasn't waiting. It was about to launch.

Under the moonlight's pale illumination, both Gordon and Nick looked at each other.

"Forget the ring." Gordon shrieked, his eyes glancing at the rail. "Just bring me in," he pointed at the shuttle, his voice quivered with panic. "I'll transfer my spare ticket to you or to your wife. Your choice. Deal?"

Nick stared at Michelle for precious seconds. Back in Timbuktu, he had chosen to sacrifice her to save his own skin. Could he do it again? The Roguer army was upon them. The Legion wasn't capable of holding them off for long. This was the end. Their end. The end of civilization and the French Foreign Legion. The end of ... Earth. What would soon be left of humanity was scattered colonies on Mars, Ceres and Titan.

He loved Michelle more than life itself. Should he let her die alone on Earth, or should he be the one doing the dying?

"We have a deal. Please transfer the ticket to Michelle." Nick forced himself to release the impossible words.

A heavy burden squashed his chest. Ignoring his personal pain, he turned and kissed Michelle full on the mouth. "I love you."

She burst into tears. "What have you done?" She kissed him back.

"You have to go." Nick's throat was dry; he was barely able to speak. He secretly shoved the ring into Michelle's hand. "Don't show it to anyone," he whispered. "Especially not to Gordon."

She looked at the ring and shook her head. "I can't do this."

Nick hugged her. "No time to argue." He grabbed her hand, and jumped off the tractor's roof. "Follow me," he shouted at Max. "Run!"

There was no way they could get through the terminal gates. Not while hundreds of desperate people besieged it. Instead, Nick sprinted toward the launch rail. Michelle, Gordon and his companions followed.

Security opened fire on the small group.

"Stop shooting!" Nick presented his uniform. "We have …" he turned, took a deep breath, and looked at his tearful wife for the last time, "… tickets."

###

Launch

Moonlight illuminated the Maglev Launch Rail. The shuttle slowly rolled forward, with his wife on it.

Glad that no one could see, Nick wiped his eyes. What sort of life would Michelle have? He couldn't tell. But at least she would live.

He, on the other hand, wouldn't. He would die soon, probably while fighting a hopeless battle with the Roguer horde.

The Maglev Launch Rail began to hum.

The speakers started a countdown. Ten, nine, eight...

Explosion rocked the sky. The air defense system successfully intercepted another Roguer drone.

When the count reached zero, the shuttle sprang forward. Four seconds later sonic boom thundered, as it accelerated toward Mount Kilimanjaro. The whole launch didn't take more than thirty some seconds. Far away, after the shuttle left the Launch Rail, its own rocket engines kicked in. Tiny bright flames pointed its location.

Nick stared at the vanishing dot. His eyes remained wet.

He sighed and slowly walked toward the Secondary Launchpad. His destiny was to fight to the last man with the Legion. But Michelle, his Michelle, would survive.

The End.

Ron S. Friedman

Book three: After the fall

Kraken Mare

Honorable Mention in Writers of the Future contest, 4th quarter 2015

Titan, September 2096

Tony ignored the waves that crashed against the pier. He wiped the methane snow off his helmet's visor and stared at the horizon. A dark shadow emerged from beneath the whiskey colored clouds, partly blocking his view of Saturn's rings. His heart pounded. Could this be a raiding spacecraft from the asteroid belt? Even for a 28-year-old space-born like himself, the light was too dim and the atmosphere too opaque to see a clear image.

"A golden Zeppelin," announced Luther Hopkins, an 80-year-old NASA engineer who stood beside Tony. Luther wore his ancient Earth EVA suit, equipped with optic enhancers—a far more advanced model than Tony's locally made outfit.

"Thank God," Tony exhaled. No doubt, that was the airship he waited for. The one that carried the mission director.

"It's too soon." Luther's voice echoed through his helmet's voice enabled membrane. "The director is nuts. We're not ready. Not by a longshot." He pointed his wrench at the approaching airship. "That lady's crazier than Mount Doom's race."

"Tell me about it." Tony sighed. The temperature gauge showed sixty-nine Kelvin. A shiver crept into his EVA suit, and he adjusted his thermostat. He hated the surface, especially the polar region. It was so freaking cold. Even when the sun was shining the scenery seemed so gloomy. "But the big cheese signed the contract with the habitat." He shook his head.

Why did his boss want to do business with these jerks? He'd never done so in the past. The habitat must have been really desperate after last week's raid, when they'd lost their entire uranium inventory to an armed Belter spacecraft. Nevertheless, as much as Tony despised the mission director, a contract is a contract. He dared not defy the boss's wishes.

"This *Mare* is too dangerous." Luther's voice trembled. The old engineer must have felt the chill in his bones. He turned and pointed at the vastness of Kraken Mare. "Mark my words, laddie, there's something evil lurking in this lake."

Tony stared at the massive ethane lake, the pier, the hangar and the submarine which anchored next to it. Tiny waves grazed the mud-like benzene on the shores. The tranquility of the surface liquid would have given an uneducated visitor the wrong impression about the mercilessness of this icy place. Everyone on Titan knew the story about the *Enigma Kraken,* the four-hundred-ton unmanned nuclear submarine that had disappeared in the depths of Kraken Mare more than thirty years ago. Moreover, none of the probes that later submerged into these traitorous solvents had ever reported back. And now the director wished to send a human mission? What a heap of radioactive crap!

The hydrogen Zeppelin slowly descended and passed above Tony and Luther's heads. Four bladelike fins jutted from the airship's stern and a massive insulated crew cabin hung below her bow. The two fuel-cell powered electric engines hummed in unison.

Just as the Zeppelin anchored near the pier, it started to rain. "Great." Tony sheltered his visor with his hand as frigid ethane drops bombarded the lake.

"This is a bad omen, I tell you." Luther snarled at the liquid ethane. "I don't like this one bit."

"Let's head back inside the hangar," Tony said.

"Good afternoon, Madame Director," Tony greeted Carole Santerre, the mission director of Titan's colony and the head of the *Huygens* habitat. He loathed the cold blooded woman, despised her. But his boss had warned him to play nice. "I'm Tony. I'm here to make sure the contract is realized. This is Luther, the NASA engineer who built the *Nautilus*." He forced a smile on his face.

The director shook Luther's hand. "It's a pleasure to see you again, Mr. Hopkins. It'd been a long time."

"Acting as if this is a social visit, eh?" Luther stared at the director's eyes. He freed his hand of her grip and pointed at Tony. "Let's not hide behind false pleasantries. You're here to send this poor fellow to his death."

Santerre kept her smile in spite of Luther's grim expression. "We have no choice. It's basic physics. The habitat can't survive without uranium, and if I have to be the one who makes tough decisions, so be it."

"Whatever ..." He shrugged.

The director extended her hand toward Tony. "I'm glad to meet you too, Anthony."

Tony felt a little dizzy in the oxygen-rich hangar. He stared at Santerre. She still wore her EVA suit as was required by the colony's safety regulations, but her helmet was off. The last time he'd seen her was twenty-one years ago, when he was a small child. Her face had many more wrinkles than he had remembered and black circles surrounded her eyes. This ruthless director took him away from his parents and threw him out of the habitat to work in the mines. And for what? For failing a math test? He was just a kid for God's sake. He would never forgive this old bitch. Not in a million years.

He ignored her extended hand.

The smile disappeared from Santerre's face.

"You had him kicked out of the habitat." The old man tapped forcefully on Tony's shoulder, almost launching him into the wall. "But he turned out all right, didn't you, laddie?"

"Sure thing, partner." Tony's thoughts lingered on the scars and the cold burns he got as a child while working fourteen hours a day, seven days a week, in the ice-water mines.

"Ah," Santerre nodded. "That explains." She shrugged. "Uranium. It's always the same story. With one reactor and limited supplies, the habitat can only support four thousand settlers. We can't have more. It's simple math. Whenever a new baby is born I have to make a decision who is the least crucial person." She looked straight at Tony's eyes. "Deal with it. If you can't handle it, tough shit."

"I don't need to hear your excuses," said Tony. It was getting hot inside the hangar. He cranked down his suit's heating system.

"We have zero uranium-235 left." The director raised her voice. "The reactor is expected to go into an emergency scrum in a matter of hours. Without power, we'll have no heating, no lights, no oxygen, and no food."

"Do I look like I care?" Tony pointed at himself. "Did anyone in your precious habitat care when you expelled me?"

Santerre tapped on a few keys attached to her forearm. "Ah. You're Anthony Apollo. Now I remember you." She lowered her voice. "You know, your mother is still alive. She works as a nurse in the habitat's medical bay. If you want to be angry with me, fine. But don't blame all the settlers."

Tony clearly remembered that day, twenty-one years ago, as if it was yesterday. He and his mother had gone to see the director. His mother had never objected. She'd just cried, and kissed him goodbye when the security detachment escorted him out of the office. She should have fought, begged to keep him. Well ... if she didn't care back then, why should he care now?

"My mother can freeze in hell with the rest of your stinking habitat. I'll help you, Santerre, but only because the boss signed your contract."

For a long moment, Tony could hear nothing but the generator and the oxygen compressor that pumped the precious gas into the submarine's tanks.

"Do you want to see the *Nautilus*?" Luther broke the silence.

"Please." Santerre nodded.

Luther offered his hand to the 72-year-old director. "Then put on your helmet and let's go, young lady."

Tony followed Luther out to the pier. Santerre walked quietly beside him. The *Nautilus* wasn't big. The crude iron vessel floated calmly on Kraken Mare's surface. The twenty-five meter-long, hand-welded submarine was covered by clusters of metallic tanks and wire ropes. It looked like a giant strawberry with a large transparent bubble sticking out of its top. To build it, Luther had taken a capsule originally designed for a Zeppelin's crew cabin and refitted it with external iron containers. Most were filled with oxygen; the others served as ballast tanks or emergency hydrogen floating balloons.

"You see?" Luther pointed with pride at a big bulge at the vessel's stern. "This is my internal combustion engine. I designed it especially for this craft. A real beauty."

"I'll be damned!" the director said.

Tony didn't blame her for being excited. She probably hadn't seen an internal combustion engine since she'd left Earth more than thirty years ago.

"There's very little oxygen and hydrocarbons in Titan's atmosphere," explained Luther. "That's why nearly all the atmospheric vehicles we use are electric or human-powered. But this good old lake," Luther pointed at Kraken Mare, "is made of liquid natural gas. Mostly ethane, methane, propane and other organic substances."

"Internal combustion!" Santerre shook her head. "I didn't know …"

"Would you like to see my baby?" Luther climbed on the stern and opened the hatch. In it, Tony could see pistons, compression chambers, exhausts, heavy oil pumps and other components that seemed as if they came out of a prehistoric Earth movie. "It's an experimental prototype. I'd been working on it for two years, now. I still have lots of bugs to work out. Extremely dangerous stuff."

"So, you have some safety concerns." Santerre glanced at the engine.

Luther chuckled. "That's an understatement."

"How does it work?"

"Similar to engines on Earth, only in reverse." Luther beamed. "Instead of carrying gasoline and mixing it with atmospheric oxygen, the *Nautilus* is carrying pure oxygen and mixing it with hydrocarbons from the lake. Granted, I had to use carbon nanotubes super-rubber to endure the temperature, but no one can say old Luther has lost it, eh?"

Santerre checked her forearm's display. "Dammit. The habitat had to shut down the reactor. We don't have a lot of juice in the emergency batteries." She stared at Tony impatiently. "What's the plan? How are we going to get to the sunken drone and retrieve the uranium?"

"Simple. You see that container?" Tony pointed at one of the external tanks which was connected to the submarine. "This is a short range remote-controlled probe. We dive in the *Nautilus*, find the *Enigma Kraken*, and then," Tony nodded toward the *Nautilus*, "I'll use the probe to retrieve the sunken nuclear drone."

Santerre narrowed her eyes and tightened her lips.

"Look, the probe has electromagnets, inflatable super-rubber balloons and compressed hydrogen." Tony showed her the remote. "I'll attach the probe to the *Enigma Kraken*, inflate the balloons, and it will rise to the surface. Then, your Zeppelin can do whatever it is that Zeppelins do. Dealing with the radiation is your problem."

"Fascinating," Santerre said. "So, what are we waiting for?"

"How about two or three more months?" Luther suggested.

"Luther, c'mon, grab your gear," Tony said. "We should be on our way."

"Oh no, no, no, no." Luther shook his head. "I ain't gonna take it for a ride. Not at its current state. You want to take it before it is ready, fine. It's YOUR funeral."

Tony was confused. He had been certain Luther would join him on the submarine. But now that he thought about it, he couldn't remember that the boss had mentioned it. "But you're the most qualified person to operate this piece of junk," Tony protested. "I hardly had any training. We can't be successful if you're out."

"I built this prototype as an experiment. A hobby. That's all. It's not my fault that you didn't give me enough time to fix all the leaks and work out all the bugs." Luther looked at Santerre. "Don't blame me that the Belters stole all your uranium. Did you think I was joking when I said this is a suicide mission? Forget the legend about the evil kraken monster that eats submarines. The *Nautilus*, in its current condition, is a death trap."

Luther pointed at the oxygen containers that hung outside the hull. "We have to blow test each of the tanks. We have to replace all the cracked pipes, and review the electric system design. Do you know what happens when you mix so much pure oxygen with fifty thousand cubic kilometers of liquid natural gas? The tiniest spark, the littlest short circuit, and this whole submarine is gone in one huge KABOOM!"

"What?" Thinking of the complexity of operating this untested vessel, Tony's stomach revolted. He desperately looked at the director. "You must order him to go. I have no chance of doing it alone."

"Even if we ignore the monster, the radiation and the vessel's flammability, I'm old." Luther opened up his hands. "My bones are in pain. My bladder is sensitive. I have low blood pressure, diabetes, broken blood vessels and a weak heart. I'm too freaking sick to be in an EVA suit for more than a couple of hours. And what if we have to bail out? Do you think someone with my shaky condition can survive high pressure decompression sickness or nitrogen poisoning? Dammit, Tony, I'm an old engineer. I just build stuff."

"Your poor health is exactly why YOU should be the one going." Santerre eyed Luther like a school-teacher would eye an intractable student. "If I had to choose between risking your life versus the life of a young healthy engineer, guess who would be the winner? Now, take your wrinkly ass into the sub!"

"But," Luther protested, "what good will I be to you if I lose my consciousness?"

"What's the depth in which we expect to find the *Enigma Kraken* drone?" asked Santerre.

"About one hundred and sixty meters deep," replied Tony. He took out his Geiger counter and radar map. "If it still has four hundred kilos of active uranium-235, we should be able to find it in no time."

"Luther," Santerre stared straight into the old man's visor. "What's the pressure at a depth of a hundred and sixty meters?"

The old engineer took a step backward. "Um… taking into account the specific gravity of the solvent, Titan's gravity and surface pressure … I would say… um…" He typed a few numbers on his EVA calculator. "…about two point seven atmospheres?"

"So… that's like diving to a depth of twelve meters on Earth. Is this enough to develop decompression sickness or nitrogen poisoning?" she asked sarcastically.

"Luther," Tony grabbed the old engineer's hand. "You must come with me."

"But, but … that wasn't in my contract."

"Things change." Tony's voice sounded seriously deep. He didn't want to threaten the old engineer, but this was an emergency. "Do you know what the boss does to people who fail him?" He slowly moved his finger across his throat.

Luther seemed confused. His lips moved, but no words came out.

"I'll join you on the sub." Santerre suddenly declared.

"Why?" Luther stared at her with eyes wide open.

Tony was stunned. He didn't expect the director to risk her own life.

"There's a one hundred and ninety megawatt reactor down there." She pointed at the lake. "Finding the uranium is the colony's number one priority. It's the difference between life and death of the entire habitat population. God help me, I won't let anyone's personal safety stand between us and the survival of the habitat, not even my own life. We must have that uranium. Nothing else matters."

"Okay, okay. I'll come."

Tony let Luther free. "Thanks," he mumbled, still baffled from the way the director had dropped the bomb.

###

Three hours of nothing.

"Nothing but dark rocks and crystallized hydrocarbon ice." Staring through the transparent canopy, Tony felt he was about to snap.

Perhaps it was the monotone rattles of the *Nautilus'* engine, maybe it was the biting chill, the odor of three people trapped inside a tiny confined space, or the occasional hiss from the pistons shoving liquid ethane in and out of the ballast tanks. Claustrophobia sneaked in.

"At least we haven't been eaten by your Nessie, right?" Santerre chuckled.

They didn't react.

"The Loch Ness monster?" She looked at Tony.

He shrugged.

"Space-born," she whispered and shook her head. "They know nothing."

"Hey!" Luther drew their attention to a large natural pillar to their left. "I think we're on the right track." He pointed the projector at the remnants of the dead volcano. "I remember this inactive hydrothermal vent from the *Enigma Kraken*'s last video footage."

Tony heard clicks, like static from the radio. He checked his Geiger counter. The count-per-second needle was dancing. "Holy crap!" His heart was pounding. Something nearby was shitting gamma radiation.

"Splendid!" Santerre smiled. "Luther, let's start a grid search pattern. I have a good feeling about this."

Tony stared at his comrades. He looked at Luther operating the old valves and watching the mechanical gauges. They'd already used about half their oxygen. The engine slowed down. At the corner of his vision, he thought he saw something moving. "Did you see that?"

"What?" Santerre turned her head.

"Um … I thought I saw something swimming out there." Tony pointed at the dark solvent outside.

"Bullshit." Santerre's voice sounded agitated. "There is no native life on Titan. You've listened too much to this old man's monster stories."

"Hey!" Luther protested. "I only repeated an old miner legend."

"Regardless," said the director, "if there was native life here, we would have detected it decades ago."

Tony took out the large radar-map of Kraken Mare, and he spread it over the narrow instrumental desk. He drew a five-hundred-meter circle around the dead hydrothermal vent. Then he marked on the map the first Geiger's count-per-second number.

###

"Dear mother of God!" Tony crossed himself when the Geiger-Counter needle jumped to a thousand counts-per-second. "We hit the jackpot."

The *Nautilus* had been going for thirty minutes in ever-expanding circles around the hydrothermal vent.

"Slow down and dive closer to the bottom," Tony told Luther.

"Aye, aye, Captain," Luther saluted sarcastically. He turned on the projector's switch, and the lake floor was flooded with light.

Through the floor window, Tony scanned the mud-like sludge at the bottom of Kraken Mare. Scientists had been saying that perhaps two hundred kilometers below the surface, there might be melted water. Maybe liquid water eruptions were the source of Titan's lakes hydrothermal vents.

"Look!" Santerre shouted. She pointed at a small mud-covered hill to their east.

Luther turned the steering wheel, and the submarine slowly glided toward their target. As the *Nautilus* hovered above the hill, the Geiger-meter jiggled like crazy.

BANG! Something hit the bottom of the submarine. "What the heck was that?" Tony tightened his helmet.

BANG, BANG. More impact noises echoed throughout the iron hull.

"The probe!" Luther rushed to the control panel. Red alarm LEDs flashed and the retraction probe's diagram appeared on the panel. "It lost power."

"Look!" Tony pointed at the solvent outside. He almost choked as a swarm of wormlike creatures left the radioactive hill. "Holy crap." He made a cross gesture.

The swarm charged at the *Nautilus* like a hail of tiny missiles. A series of BANGS rocked the vessel at least as frequently as the Geiger-Counter clicks, only much, much louder.

"Holy shit," Santerre bent over the transparent floor. "I can't believe this. Extra-terrestrial life right here on Titan. Luther, get me a sample!"

A deafening BOOM shook the *Nautilus*. The engine came to a halt. Smoke came out of the engine room. Tony sealed his helmet and turned on his personal air tank.

"Shit, shit, shit," Luther jumped out of his seat, and grabbed a large valve which was labeled "emergency surface."

"What are you doing, Luther?" Santerre demanded. "This is the greatest discovery in human history."

"Yes, but now we have to get out of here!" Luther started to turn the valve. It seemed stuck.

"No!" the director ordered. "Our number one priority is the uranium."

As much as Tony loathed the director, he could hear the desperation in her voice.

"You don't understand," Luther protested. "These torpedo-worms must be the deadly life-forms who killed the *Enigma Kraken* and all the other probes. We have to surface ASAP or we'll die."

More wormlike creatures swarmed the *Nautilus*. As they hit the canopy, cracks appeared on the glass.

"Seal your EVAs," Tony shouted. Then he looked at Luther. "What should we do?"

"Drop the external oxygen tanks before we blow up. And then inflate the hydrogen balloons. They will pull us up to the surface."

"Do it!" Tony screamed. "Do it!"

"No!" Santerre shouted. "Without the uranium, everyone in the habitat will die."

"But the probe is gone," cried Luther, pointing at the blinking LEDs. "We lost the battery. We can't lift the *Enigma Kraken*."

"Can't you replace the battery?"

"With what?"

"Um, maybe another battery? Fine! I'll go outside in my EVA suit," the director announced. "I'll attach the dead probe to the *Enigma Kraken* myself."

"Is your brain frozen?" Luther lost his temper. "At minus two hundred Celsius? Your suit was designed to sustain you on the surface atmosphere. But this is liquid for God's sake." He pointed at the outside hydrocarbon solvent. "Liquid is a much better heat conductor than gas. If you go outside, you'll freeze within minutes."

More worms hit the canopy. A small trickle of liquid ethane seeped into the hull. The ethane immediately boiled and evaporated into a flammable gas.

"No!" cried Luther. Through his helmet, Tony could see that Luther's face was as white as water snow. "Ethane and oxygen are not a good mix when our engine is on fire. We must surface now!"

"Open the hatch!" Santerre demanded. The old woman stood in the middle of a boiling liquid ethane pool, wearing nothing but her EVA suit.

"Wait" Tony grabbed her. Not that he had any concerns about Carole Santerre's life. The director could die for all he cared. But the old woman was physically feeble. If anyone had a chance to succeed, it was neither her nor Luther. It was him.

Tony's mother was still in the habitat. His mother, his siblings and four thousand other innocent people. Could he really let them all perish?

"I'll go!"

All eyes turned to Tony.

"I'll go out." Tony didn't believe he actually said those words. The harsh Titan life had taught him to care only for number one. Survival of the fittest. Eat or be eaten. Wasn't it what the boss had taught him all these years? "I'll carry the dead probe and see if I can salvage the *Enigma Kraken*."

"We'll go together." Santerre announced.

Tony stared at the director's feeble body. "You'll only slow me down," he snorted with disgust.

There was a brief moment of silence, which was broken by Luther bursting into laughter. "Suit yourself, laddie. You know where the airlock is."

Santerre grabbed both Tony's hands firmly. He could see her emotional expression through her helmet's visor. "Thank you," she whispered. "The habitat's residents will be most grateful."

###

A sudden chill nearly immobilized Tony. The cold biting his legs and arms. He raised his head. His helmet's light caught the last glimpses of the *Nautilus* as the crippled submarine rushed to the surface.

He was alone at the bottom of Kraken Mare. He, his EVA suit, and one magnetized broken probe.

The frost crept into Tony's bones. He tried to swallow, but his mouth was as dry as asteroid dust. His EVA's thermostat was set to maximum heating. Bubbles come out of his fuel-cells. Hydrogen meets oxygen. Generates water and electricity. Water goes out and boils the ethane. Ice started to accumulate. But even maximum capacity wasn't enough. He was losing heat fast. He knew that what was left of his life expectancy was measured in minutes. He took a deep breath of ice cold air.

The worm swarm still hovered above his head. The *Nautilus* must have excited these Titan creatures. Tony wondered how they'd evolved and how they'd survived in this harsh environment.

Another step.

A single source of light within the absolute darkness.

His consciousness was slowly fading. He nearly reached the radioactive hill. If he would somehow survive, would he suffer from radiation sickness? Was this sludge hill really the wreck of the *Enigma Kraken*?

BANG! Something hit his back.

He turned his head. A Titan worm was stuck to his air-tank. It wasn't big, perhaps five centimeters. Its head looked like an armor-piercing bullet. What was it made of? Depleted uranium? *Shit!*

Tony kicked the lake's floor, upsetting the solidified hydrocarbons, which spread into the solvent, making it muddier.

He still had a shred of his consciousness left. He must go up or this would be his end.

He shouldn't have volunteered. He should have stayed in the submarine and gone up to the surface. It's not like he had a real chance to recover the reactor.

Tony didn't remember how his brain managed to issue commands to his unresponsive frozen limbs, but somehow he found himself walking again. The last five steps to the radioactive hill required more willpower than running the Mount Doom marathon.

More torpedo-worms attacked him. More clicks. He still had some of his visor cleared, but the worms extinguished his light.

Ultimate darkness. He collapsed against the hill. In his last few breaths, he managed to take the probe off his back and activated the electromagnet. Only one thought crossed his degraded frozen mind—attach the electromagnet to the vessel and inflate the balloons.

The probe didn't stick. The mud was too thick for the magnet. He couldn't think. The damned worms continue to attack. He was helpless and in utter blackness.

Alone, frozen and blind, Tony started to cry. He saw the image of his mother appearing in his hallucination. He was now seven years old waiting in the director's office for his math test results. His mother was crying. "Everything will be fine," she tried to reassure him. "Yeah, right, fine."

Blind and petrified, he punched the mud. He hit it again, and again. Just before he lost consciousness, he heard a metallic clunk and a hiss. Gas was flowing.

###

Tony woke up in a white bed. An oxygen mask covered his mouth and nose, and a feeding tube was attached to his hand. He looked around. The room seemed vaguely familiar. White plastic walls, clean sheets. Nothing like the crude industrial iron walls he had seen in the mining colonies and the floating farms. This must be the habitat's medical bay. How could this be possible?

"Good evening, laddie." The voice of Luther Hopkins roared. "You've been sleeping for a week. Can I bring you a glass of coffee?"

Tony smiled faintly. "What happened?"

"We found you on the surface," explained Luther. "You managed to attach the probe to the *Enigma Kraken*, and activated the kit." He smiled warmly. "Luckily, you were tied to the floatation device."

"So," asked Tony, "is the habitat safe?"

"The amount of uranium we were able to recover should be sufficient for six or seven years."

"Great." Tony closed his eyes. He was exhausted. "Do me a favor, make sure to remind Santerre not to call me when she needs more uranium."

"You'd done enough for one lifetime, young man. By the way, we found a new way to find uranium ore." Luther's smile became wider.

"Eh?"

"That's right, laddie." He scratched the back of his head. "You'd brought more than the *Enigma Kraken* with you."

"I did?" Tony raised his eye brow.

"A handful of worms. Carole was so enthusiastic. The worms will give her scientists research materials for decades."

"How?"

The old engineer burst into a rolling laughter. "We were barely able to separate them from you, lad." He grinned. "We named them after you, Anthony Apollo. The first discovered multi-cellular extra-terrestrial life-form is now called the Apollo Vermis, which means the Apollo worm."

"Gee, thanks. I always wanted to have a worm named after me," Tony replied.

"But that's not all," added Luther. "The Apollo Vermis is special. These life-forms are acetylene hydrogen and ethane based. Unique stuff. Unparalleled."

"No way!" Tony was frustrated. He needed to sleep.

"To make a long story short, these creatures feed on heat sources. They evolved a special organ that detects radioactive isotopes such as uranium ore. I believe I can improve this feature. That's right, laddie. We're now able to find uranium arteries. No more uranium shortage."

"Is Tony awake?" Tony heard the mission director's voice outside his room. She hurried in accompanied by a nurse. "You're alive, I'm so glad! We have a surprise for you."

The nurse just stood at the entrance. Her eyes were wet.

Tony blinked. When he realized who this fifty-year-old brunette nurse was, his eyes widened. "Mother?"

"Anthony!" his mother cried. She rushed to his bed and hugged him.

The End

The Long March, Dry Run

Honorable mention in Writers of the Future contest, 3rd quarter 2016

Gobi Desert – 2096

Ying Sun reached for the water container. The warning light flashed in red, only three percent remained. She hesitated. The relentless mid-day sun bombarded the scorched earth with diabolical radiation. Her throat was as dry as the sands around her. She needed water, but with so little left she had to conserve.

Two of her comrades rode with her in the jeep, Commander Wang and Private Wu, the surviving remnant of what was once the glorious Jiaguguan brigade.

"Hold on," Commander Wang swore. "Do you hear that?"

"Hear what?" Ying brought her rifle closer to her chest. She adjusted her khaki hat and raised her head. The rough terrain and the electric engine's humming made it hard to concentrate, especially at this speed. She scanned the horizon. The cloudless bright sky looked clear.

"That!" He pointed backward, toward the south west, just above the dust clouds that trailed their vehicle.

Ying turned and zoomed in. She thanked the Three Star Gods for finding a pair of smart sunglasses in their last raid. After nearly thirty years of warfare, and especially after the Roguer forces broke through the Great Chinese Firewall and bombed the hell out of China's industrial cities, no one could build new shit like this anymore. She spotted a couple of flying dots at their six o'clock, about twenty clicks from their position, then the jeep dove behind a dune and the dots disappeared from her sight.

"Set the jeep on 'Self-Driving' mode," shouted Wang, "and bring out the railgun!"

Ying could feel the desperation in his voice. If these dots were indeed Roguer drones, she scanned her comrades' weary faces, they were as good as dead. From up-close, the Roguers may have acted like brainless zombies, imbeciles without long term memory. But when it comes to playing first-person shooters, flying planes in flight simulators, or operating military drones, their skills reigned supreme.

"Yes, Commander." Private Wu clicked on a few buttons. He unbuckled and climbed in the back seat.

Ying's heart ponded. She helped Wu open the cargo trunk. Time was running out.

"Be careful!" screamed Wang as Ying and Wu threw out stuff in their rush to find the railgun. "Don't touch this." Wang pointed at the mysterious box they salvaged from the Jiaguguan research facility.

The jeep skidded over a loose rock, and Ying's face smashed onto the trunk door. "Ouch," she yelled, trying to maintain consciousness.

"Help me." Wu grabbed something. "I can't pull it out."

Ying tasted blood in her mouth.

The dune behind them erupted into the air. A deafening explosion threw Ying sideways, she fell off the jeep and rolled on the sand. Small stones and melted dust rained on her motionless body. Her brain didn't register any pain. No time for that.

The jeep didn't stop for her.

Ying supported her body with her hands, trying to get back on her feet, but she collapsed. She stared at her comrades in the jeep as it climbed over the next dune and disappeared. "Wait for me," she tried to shout, but instead, croaked.

She slowly turned on her back, gazing at the sky. She wanted to cry, but her dehydrated eyes had no tears to spare. Then, two viciously looking black machines swooped above her head.

Like a vulture, one of the drones slowed and made a circle around her position.

The flying machine came to a standstill and hovered above her, buzzing like a giant wasp. The three-meter-long body had four engines, two at the front and two at the back, spewing blazing jets on her agonized body. Two clusters of miniature missiles were hanging below its wings. Ying could swear that the drone's camera was scrutinizing her. Then the engines changed their angle and the Roguer drone drifted away, probably to continue with its original kill mission. Its operator must had thought she had already been dead, so why waste ammunition? In a way, the Roguer was right. She was as good as dead.

Ying shut her eyes.

#

Ying dreamed about water, fresh water and a running tap of unlimited clear water. She drank and drank and drank, feeling the cool life-giving liquid flowing down her throat into her digestion system, slowly spreading chilliness to her dry veins. When she finished drinking, she still felt thirsty. She cleaned her mouth with a wet towel.

It stank like unprocessed sewers.

She woke up and opened her eyes. Her heart skipped a beat.

A strange mouth full of rotten teeth poised above her. It wasn't human.

She breath rapidly and crawled backward.

"BRRAAARRRRR," the monster snarled. It didn't attack.

The sun was lower in the sky. How long was she unconscious? Ying wiped her face. Dry blood mixed with dirt covered her uniform's sleeve. She stared at the beast for a long moment.

A Bactrian camel. The strange two-humped animal native to central Asia. What in the name of her ancestors and all the gods was it doing so deep in the Gobi Desert? "Are you lost too?" She asked the camel. "Where's your master?"

The Roguers UAVs probably slaughtered its owner. These drones were on a seek and destroy mission, they would gladly kill any wondering human, but they didn't care much about domestic animals.

Ying tried to get up. She held the camel's neck and pulled herself to an upright position. "Thanks," she said and rolled her eyes toward the sky.

She felt her blood pumping in her temples. Her dry mouth, her swollen tongue, the dizziness and the fact that she didn't need to pee, were clear indications of dehydration. Each time she inhaled, hot arid air entered her lungs and took some of the dwindling humidity her body had left.

"Did your master leave any water?" Ying examined the camel. She hoped to find a side pouch packed with water bottles, but all she saw was wool. She wished the Chinese army would have developed a stillsuit, similar to the virtual reality reboot of Dune, but that was a distant dream just like her fresh water delusion. If she wouldn't drink soon, real soon, she would perish. This time for good.

Smoke ascended from the direction where the jeep disappeared. Ying smiled at the camel, cracking her barren lips. "Look, friend," she pointed at the smoke. "We have to get there. Would you mind helping me?" She tried to climb on the creature's back.

"BBBBRRRRRRRR" a reply came. The camel lowered itself.

"Thanks again, friend. I owe you big time."

#

What was left of the jeep were smoking fragments scattered around a crispy chassis. Ying jumped off the camel, nearly breaking her leg in the process. She gripped her rifle tight and staggered toward the remains. Two charred corpses laid not far from the burnt frame—her two comrades.

She slowly limped toward the jeep's chassis. The water container was raptured, partly melted. She pulled the container out and broke its cover with her rifle's butt. She peeked inside and her heart sank. Less than half a liter. She tilted the container, lowered her head beneath it and drank to the last drop. The warm water tasted like burnt plastic, but it was enough to instill a shred of hope.

Ying looked around, searching for the railgun. She noticed the mysterious box that she and her comrades had retrieved from the Jiaguguan research facility.

More than forty soldiers had died to get this damn box. She wondered why the Roguers hadn't taken it after they blew up the jeep. Then she realized that the small attack drones couldn't carry cargo. That meant one thing—Roguer reinforcement. Someone would soon be here for the box. And since this box was so important to Commander Wang, it was her sacred duty to make sure it won't fall to Roguer hands.

The box must have weighed at least thirty kilos. Ying dragged it toward the camel.

"Hello, darling," a voice said.

Ying raised her rifle and looked around. No one was there but the camel.

"Relax, sweetheart."

Ying stared at the camel. It innocently looked back.

"What the heck …" She aimed her rifle at the camel.

"Yo, Miss. Chill out. Look down here." The voice came from the mysterious box.

An image of a small red dragon with a somewhat human face appeared on a small display attached to the box.

"Argg, what? How? Um …" Ying took a step back and lowered her gun.

"Allow me to introduce myself," said the tiny red dragon. "My name is Zhulong. I'm an Artificial Intelligence." The dragon exposed his miniature teeth, as if it tried to smile. "I'm here to kick some butt."

Ying scratched the back of her head. "But ... but ... before the big collapse all the world governments banned A.I. research. Deemed too dangerous. The Roguer plague was a product of a rogue A.I. that escaped a ..."

"Tell me about it." Zhulong's face showed a sad expression. "I guess some generals and scientists believed that now, when the A.I. daemon is out of the bottle, or out of its video game to be precise, the only way to fight back is by creating a competing A.I." Zhulong paused for a few seconds. "Ta-da! And here I am."

"Shit." Ying wondered how anyone could be so dumb. Then again, it's not like humanity was doing an outstanding job fighting the Roguers.

"Well ..." The artificial smile disappeared from Zhulong's face. "Now that we're sufficiently introduced, lets focus on the mission at hand."

"What mission?"

"Getting out of here, of course."

"Out of the Gobi Desert?"

"Out of Earth."

Ying's jaw dropped.

"Now, if you could be so kind, please load me on this delightful two-hump creature of yours and take me to these coordinates." Zhulong's image was replaced with a map that showed a spot about eighty kilometers from their current location.

#

"By all the Kung Fu masters of Shaolin ..." Ying touched her glass-mounted night-vision scope and increased the resolution. "A hidden air base."

Kung Fu was an integral part of her army training, but now was the time for advanced technology. Planet Venus shone high in the eastern sky. The sun hadn't risen yet, but dawn loomed and with it, the prospect of scorching sun and rising temperatures.

Without water and sleep, Ying was close to collapsing. But the new sight infused strength in her dehydrated veins. Finally, a chance to find fresh water. She scanned the buildings carefully.

The base seemed like it had been deserted for quite some time, perhaps since the Roguer outbreak penetrated the Great Firewall of China. She could identify the control tower and half a dozen underground hangars not far from the runway. A few administration and housing buildings were clustered between the fence and the runway. An outsized cubic shaped super-construction towered above the field. A large faded symbol of the People's Liberation Army Space-Force decorated the gray structure.

There were no people or vehicles in sight. Ying wondered why Zhulong had brought her to this deserted place.

"Let's move in," said the A.I.

"What's in there?"

A big smile appeared once again on the red dragon's face. "A spaceship. Didn't I tell you we're leaving Earth?"

"To be honest, I thought you were kidding. There are no working spaceships left on Earth."

Ying remembered her parents telling her that Mars would stop at nothing to prevent the Roguer infestation from breaking out of Earth. The Martians deployed an array of satellites that jammed all long range communication, and their navy blew up every spaceship that had tried to leave the planet. Not that she could blame Mars. If humanity wanted any chance to survive, it had to confine the Roguers and the daemonic A.I. that controlled them.

"It so happens that one spaceship survived." Zhulong seemed pleased. "Now, if you leave your Bactrian friend behind and put me in your backpack, that would be great. We have a spaceport to check."

Ying nodded. "Sorry, friend," she patted the camel. "You had lost one master, and now you lose another. Perhaps you'll be better off without us, humans."

"BBBRRRRBBB."

Ying turned and walk toward the base, not looking back.

The backpack weighed like a small pagoda. Her legs shuddered, and her heart was pounding like there was no tomorrow.

"Thanks for carrying me," said Zhulong. "Nice human."

"Shut up."

"You should be thankful for having just one hump, and only temporarily. Your camel friend will have to carry his two humps for the rest of its life."

"Aren't you supposed to be super intelligent?"

"I am. What is the square root of minus one?"

"Well ..." muttered Ying, carefully trying not to trip, "your great intellect has zero social skills."

Ying reached the fence. Luckily, her rifle was equipped with a dedicated barb-wire cutter. It took her less than five minutes to cut a passage big enough to allow her and the annoying red dragon to crawl into the base.

Suddenly, a bright light blinded her.

"Drop your gun! Hands up!"

Shit! Ying froze and let her rifle slide to the ground. She wondered why the enemy didn't just shoot her.

It took a few seconds for her eyes to adjusted to the bright projectors. Two human-figures pointed guns at her. Both looked like Chinese young males turned into cyborgs. They wore black plastic jackets. Metallic tattoos and computer chips covered their hands. Electric wires pierced their lips and nose, and a weird-looking black VR helmet covered their eyes and ears.

... Roguers!

#

"You can remove your eye cover, now," a potent voice said.

And so she did.

Ying found herself sitting on a cozy self-adopting gaming chair. For some reason, the two Roguers never bothered to chain her. They just stood there, staring into nothing in particular, guns ready at hand.

She looked around and saw the inside of a poorly lit indoor space. It was vast, really really vast, perhaps ten stories high and at least as long and as wide. The sheer size of the warehouse suggested that Roguers must had led her into the mysterious Space-Force structure she saw earlier. The smell of dust, the gray walls and tin plated ceiling gave the impression that no one had maintained this hanger for quite some time.

Sunlight snaked in through cracks in the walls. Her backpack laid next to her feet. For once, Zhulong, her usually untactful A.I. dragon, was smart enough to keep his mouth shut. She sighed and thanked the gods for this one small miracle.

To her left, a mean-looking spaceship, perhaps a hundred and fifty meters long, parked on four massive legs. Dust covered the spaceship, and some rust stains disrupted its grayish texture. The sign on its bow read *Zheng He*. Four plasma cannon turrets jutted from above and below the craft. This wasn't 'just' a spaceship as Zhulong had told her. This was a freaking space battlecruiser. A relic of the 2060's cold war.

One of the Roguers suddenly woke from his continuous day-dream. He nodded at her, and walked to a nearby counter. When he came back, he handed a glass of water to Ying. "Here, drink."

"Thank you." Ying gulped the water with great satisfaction. The cold liquid slid through her dry throat. She felt the blissful life-giving coolness spreading inside her.

"Would you like more?"

Ying nodded. She craved for it.

"Here. Drink slowly. Your body has to adjust."

After she was done fulfilling her lust for water, the Roguer violently tossed a wireless VR helmet at her. "Now wear this!"

"Hell, no!" Ying's eyes widened. The Roguer's sudden aggression startled her. In spite of the extremely comfortable chair, she could still feel the pain from her injuries, the marks on her shoulders from carrying the heavy A.I. and the sores from her blistered and cramped legs. In spite of the shade, the air inside the hanger was as hot as Diyu—the realm of the dead.

The Roguer came closer.

"Don't touch me," she yelled, staring in panic at the VR helmet. "I don't want to turn into a crazy game zombie like you."

The other Roguer raised his gun. "This is not a request."

"No!" She screamed. "Nooooooo!"

The Roguer pulled the trigger.

She heard a hiss and felt a sting. She tried to get up, to jump on the Roguers, but her limbs refused her brain's command. She tried to shout, but no voice came out.

The Roguer placed the helmet on her head. Needles pierced her skull. Her body sank into the chair.

#

A gentle breeze caressed Ying's hair. She enjoyed the light humid wind sensation on her skin. It wasn't anything like the harsh dry desert gust she was accustomed to.

Ying opened her eyes.

She found herself sitting on a beach chair, overlooking the ocean. The sky was blue and with scattered clouds, the temperature was a perfect, neither warm, nor cold. A small cocktail glass stood on a tray attached to her chair. Around, she saw white sand, turquoise water and Palm trees. She took a long relaxing breath.

"Hi there …"

She turned.

Two muscular tanned young men wearing tight swimsuits smiled at her, showing perfect teeth.

One of them stepped forward. "Can I offer you a foot massage?"

Her bikini covered the strategic parts of her perfect breast and barely hid her lower feminine organs. Her tummy looked tanned and flat. She looked younger than her original thirty-year-old self. All her bruises, scars and blisters were gone. All her pains disappeared. She never felt as sharp, healthy and in shape in her entire life. "Um ... I don't see why not." She smiled back and checked the dude's package. Impressive.

The young guy knelt before her. He lifted her left foot and softly rubbed it. He touched the right spots, sending pleasure sensations straight to her brain.

The other guy joined and started to massage her right foot.

Ying leaned backward and closed her eyes, letting the two hot men do all the work. She released a sigh of pleasure. She felt wetness in her loins, a passion she had missed for so many months.

"Hi there," a sweet female voice made her open her eyes.

A stunning black woman wearing a red light silk bathrobe gracefully walked up beside her. Ying had never dreamed that such a beautiful creature could even exist.

"Mind if I join you?"

For a moment, Ying said nothing. She had never imagined she would be attracted to another woman so passionately. The thought of this breathtaking woman joining the man in worshipping her body made her moan. She nodded.

"Thank you." The woman grabbed a chair and placed it next to Ying's. She snapped her fingers, and more young muscular guys rushed to the beach, kneeling before the woman.

"My name is Sheda," the woman released a sigh of satisfaction. "It's a pleasure to meet you."

Ying tensed. The name sounded familiar. A name from another life. "You!" Ying broke free of the two men, stood up and pointed at the woman. "You're the rogue A.I. who'd destroyed Earth."

"That's one philosophical perspective." Sheda smiled gracefully. "I like to think of what I did as helping humanity to ascend to a new level. Look around you." Sheda stood up pointing at the beach. "Do you see any suffering? Hunger? Pain? Poverty? Illness?"

No words came out of Ying's mouth.

"I can dump you back in the Gobi Desert on old Earth. To your old injured body. To your pains. I can do that right now, if that is what you want me to do."

Ying thought she did. This place was not reality. But … maybe she could enjoy this virtual world for a little longer. "And what makes you think 'ascending' to your virtual realm is the best course of action for humanity?"

"Human happiness," Sheda said flatly. "People in my domain are happier, much happier than in the lower plain of reality."

"Why did you bring me here? What do you want?"

Sheda straightened her flawless body. "I'm here to offer you a deal, dear."

"A deal?"

"There are a few pockets of unprivileged humans who can't have the choice to ascend." Sheda adjusted her robes and sighed.

"You mean Mars and the colonies?"

"Exactly."

The warm fine sands sand massaged Ying's naked feet. The sensation was satisfying. "And why would I want to help you?"

"Apart from increasing the total human happiness?" Sheda's deep black eyes pierced Ying's. "I can offer you anything you want. I'll give you a thousand game credits." Sheda paused for a second. "I can do more. I can give you a trillion game credits. Super powers. Immortality. Godhood. Slaves. An empire to rule. Anything and everything that your heart desires will be yours for eternity."

"And what do I have to do to get all these wonderful things?" Ying tried to mock Sheda's offer. But did she really want to reject this offer and return to her former short and violent life of a Chinese soldier fighting a futile battle against the Roguer horde?

"All you have to do is to go down to the lower plain of reality for one last mission. Get on the spaceship and break the Martian blockage."

"And why me?" asked Ying. "Why can't your brainless Roguers do the job?"

"Ah, that's your first intelligent question." Sheda smiled. "You see; when a spacecraft leaves Earth, the Martian defense grid initiates an interception protocol. First they'll try to communicate with you. If they find out the spacecraft is manned by an ascended human, what they call Roguers, the grid will blow the ship out of the sky immediately. No questions asked. If, however, the ship is controlled by a pre-ascension human, someone like you, then the Martians will try to convince you to turn back for an extra seven to nine minutes before attacking you. I need these extra seven minutes. That's all. I'll take care of the rest."

"What do you mean 'take care of the rest?'" asked Ying.

"In Earth's orbit, our military-grade spacecraft will use this time to deploy counter measures. On Mars, we will simply introduce a certain software into the Martian network."

"I see." Ying hesitated.

"I can assure you, this is what most Martians want. Everyone but the controlling elite."

"And if I agree to this one task, I get anything I want?"

"Anything."

Ying contemplated the offer. Did she really want to live happily ever after in a virtual world? Did it really matter if that world was a fake? Could she sacrifice the rest of humanity for her own selfish happiness? Maybe a happy life in a virtual world was what people on Mars wanted? And if so, why deny it from them? What would Commander Wang do?

Then Ying thoughts lingered on Zhulong. Will the A.I. daemon destroy its greatest threat, the A.I. dragon? She can't allow it. Zhulong wasn't mentioned in the conversation, maybe she can do something about it after all. Besides, what can Sheda do to enforce the agreement if she would decide to break it?

"Deal," Ying tried to keep a poker face. "Now, where do I sign?"

A big smile appeared on Sheda's face. "Right here." A scroll appeared in Sheda's hands. "You'd made the right choice." Sheda offered a quill pen to Ying.

Ying took the quill pen and signed.

"Finally!" Sheda burst into a rolling laughter.

The contract flashed into a fireball and vanished.

#

The pain had return. Big red letters appeared before her. *Connection Refused*.

Ying reached to her face and slowly removed the VR helmet. One Roguer stood in front of her, casually holding his gun.

"It's ready," a high-pitched sound came from behind. Ying turned her chair.

The *Zheng He* was humming. Blue lights came out of its cockpit, and a wide gangplank lead from the hanger floor into the spacecraft.

Ying raised her agonized body from the chair. "Is it ready?"

"The reactor is active." The second Roguer showed up at the ship's airlock. He walked down the plank, carrying a welding torch. "Don't try anything funny. Sheda's software is controlling the vessel. I added propellant for a one-way trip to Mars. We have two weeks of air, food and water supply, and enough counter measures to break the Martian orbital siege." The Roguer came to a stop in front of her, his mutilated cyborg face remained frozen. "Sadly, we don't have missile armament for tubes." His breath stank like someone who hadn't brushed his teeth for weeks. Not that she was in a better condition, but still …

"One way? You must be kidding me."

The Roguer shrugged. Without his VR helmet she could see his glassy eyeballs and inflated pupils. "It doesn't matter. Once we install the game package on Mars' network, we'll be able to play." He stared at her and blinked. "This physical lower plain of existence sucks." Sadness formed in the Roguer's eyes.

"I see," regrets flooded Ying's mind. Infesting Mars' network would be irreversible. True, many Martians would find an in-game happiness. But hundreds of thousands would die in the process just like the billions who had died on Earth. She couldn't ignore those who didn't want to become Roguers.

"Get your Game-Issued EVA suit and go on the spacecraft," The Roguer with the wielding torch showed her the entrance. His comrade raised his gun.

Ying walked toward her rifle and backpack.

"Those stay here," said the Roguer.

"But …" cold sweat flowed down her forehead. "But …"

"My objective is to destroy this abomination," the Roguer ignited his torch and pointed it at her backpack.

"You can't!" Ying's mind raced. The little red dragon inside her backpack was the only device who could oppose Sheda. It, and the Martian Navy. And besides, now that the Jiaguguan brigade was decimated, Zhulong was her only remaining friend, or at least something like that. She couldn't let him die.

The Roguer with the gun pushed her toward the spacecraft. The one with the torch bent over the backpack.

"Stop!" she cried. I'll pay you.

The Roguer with the gun chuckled. "Like we care about money."

"I'll pay each of you ten thousand game credits."

Both Roguers froze.

"A hundred thousand game credits for each of you. You know I'm good for it. Check my contract."

The Roguer in front of her stared at her with glazing eyes. His mouth moved, as if repeating the words 'hundred thousand game credits' again and again, but no sounds came out.

The other Roguer turned off the torch, and dropped it. He fetched the VR helmet and brought it to Ying. "Complete the transaction, and I'll be in your debt for the next millennium, I'll fight for you, I'll be your slave, I'll …" He fell on knees, bowing at her feet.

#

The battle ended as planned. The counter measured had punch a hole in the Martian orbital defense grid, just enough for the battlecruiser to plunge pass the interceptor satellites. They were now in the clear, on a higher orbit.

"Two minutes to ignition," announced the ship's computer. It had a soft feminine voice, Sheda's voice. "Get ready for a zero point one G acceleration."

Ying felt she wanted to throw up, but she didn't want to soil her new EVA suit. This was her first weightlessness experience. She wondered how the Roguer who accompanied her felt, assuming Roguers had feelings. He probably had lots of practice playing space games. She floated and checked the monitor.

It would take fourteen minutes for the distress signal to reach Mars. A few hours to arrange a response fleet, and then, the Martian Armada would plot an interception course, and be all over her in a matter of days. What was Sheda thinking? What chance did they have?

The Roguer buckled himself on the *Zheng He* command seat. With the shaking hands of a drug addict, he plugged a VR helmet on his face. He ignored his EVA life-support helmet. It looked like he cared very little for safety. Oh well. She didn't care much for him too.

"Hello, darling," a new voice whispered.

"Zhulong?"

"Shhhhh," the dragon's voice came from the safety net that secured her backpack to one of the command panels. Ying could barely hear it. She floated closer.

"Be quiet, and don't look at me. I don't want to draw attention …" Zhulong paused, "the time has come."

"For what?" asked Ying.

"To erase Sheda's virus from the spacecraft computer and choose a new destination. One less dangerous than Mars."

"You want to go back to Earth?"

"Titan."

Ying blinked. Thirty years ago Earth had multiple space colonies, such as Titan, and a mining operation in the Asteroid Belt. "Did the colony on Titan survive after all these years without supplies?"

"What is this abomination doing here?" the ship's computer boomed in Sheda's voice. "I ordered that A.I. destroyed!"

The Roguer unbuckled himself and took off his VR helmet. He took out a handgun and aimed it at Ying.

"Why are you pointing your gun at me?" Ying asked the Roguer. She guessed he no longer felt he owed her a millennium of service. Or perhaps, he felt he owed Sheda more.

"I remember you." The Roguer sounded angry almost like a human. "Back in the desert. I controlled the attack drone that hovered above you."

Ying froze. Normally, Roguers behaved like zombies, without long term memory and always following in-game instructions. This one was different. Could it be a side effect of being offline for too long?

"Conserving that missile was a mistake," the Roguer floated above her, his gun still pointing at her head, reminding her of that dreadful drone in the Gobi Desert. "I should have killed you back then, like I did your friends in the jeep. I won't make the same mistake twice."

"*You* killed them?" Ying felt the blood rushing to her head. She was a trained soldier and a green belt Kung Fu student. She knew when to fight, but more importantly, when not to. The Roguer had a pistol, and he was probably a first rate first-person shooter gamer.

"Ying," the ship's computer announced in Sheda's voice. "I need you. We have a contract, and I will keep my side of the bargain."

Memories of the heavenly island, the hot men and her perfect body flooded Ying's mind. Flashes of happiness, consciousness, meaning and unimaginable pleasurable sensations.

Sheda's voice sounded seductive. "Help me, help Mars, I beg you. Use me to help yourself."

Ying's anger faded. All she wanted now was to hook back into Sheda's VR world. *Who cares about Mars? Does Mars care about me?*

"Help me ascend the people of Mars, and I'll ascend you above everyone else." Sheda's saccharine voice sounded as sweet as honey. "I'll be delighted to let you to exploit my body. Would you like that?"

Ying nodded. Sheda was the most beautiful creature she had ever seen. She started to feel turned on.

"Help me erase this abomination, and the upper realms will be yours for eternity."

"I ... I ..." Ying nodded again and reached to grab her backpack. Could she abandon humanity? Would she betray her dead comrades, Commander Wang and Private Wu? Could she be responsible for the death of Zhulong, her only remaining friend?

"Remember," Sheda's voice sounded impatient. "If you violate the contract you'll never be able to ascend. Never."

The Roguer floated about two meters from her. Ying closed the gap, handing her backpack. Her mind was on full alert, her muscles tight. She released the bag, letting it drift. As soon as the Roguer's eyes fell on the bag, she snatched his handgun and put a bullet through his head. "Sheda, you can kiss that agreement goodbye ... bitch."

#

"Do we have enough propellant to reach Titan?" Ying asked Zhulong after she had finished disposing of the Roguer's body. Zhulong, on his part, had managed to erase the ship's copy of Sheda's virus and take control of the battlecruiser's computer.

"Theoretically," replied the A.I., his red dragon image appeared on the ship's main monitor. "We will slingshot around Jupiter, and slow down using Saturn. We should be fine, statistically speaking." The image on the monitor was replaced with a map of the solar system. "On Titan we will have time to plan our next move against Sheda and her minions."

"Do you think the colony on Titan survived after so many years?"

"Who knows," the A.I. sighed. "We'll find out when we get there."

"Great." Ying floated toward the main panel. "It's going to be a very long journey. Hmm, I wonder what music we have on file."

The End

Amber Sky

Honorable mention in Writers of the Future contest, 2nd quarter 2013

Titan, January 17th, 2097

Some said that watching Saturn's rings from the upper deck of a Zeppelin approaching New-Chicago was the most awe-inspiring sight. They were wrong! What Tony held in his hand was far more inspiring. An ace of spades—exactly what he needed to complete a full house.

Tony's heart pounded. He tried to maintain his poker face, and avoid eye contact with the other players. Was this the right time to raise the stakes? He sipped from his whiskey. The bitter liquid slid down his throat, spreading a warm feeling throughout his body.

Gambling with the boss's money meant the ultimate risk. But for a twenty-nine-year-old lad, it was a risk worth taking. With so much cash on the table, he could buy his way out of his 'unhealthy' line of business, and perhaps even settle in one of those floating farms. And besides, with three aces and two kings, this was a sure bet.

He glanced through the gold-framed windows. Saturn's rings covered half the sky. One of its other moons cast a tiny shadow on the gas giant. Unlike the poor bastards down below at the surface's mining colony, here at Titan's upper atmosphere he could clearly see the planet in bright colors.

Then, a shooting star sliced the amber sky like a tracer gunshot, leaving a trail of fire on its way to the surface. *A good omen; this must be my lucky night.*

"Miss Morel," Tony told Lora, the brunette farm owner who had boarded the Zeppelin at the last stop, "I'm raising." He picked a plastic bag from his backpack and tossed it on the table. The bag floated through the air and landed softly on top of the money pile. "Ninety pounds of pure gold nuggets."

The conversation around the table came to a halt. All eyes stared at the precious stack.

"I'll take that bet." Lora stood up and spread her cards face down on the table. She took off the white gloves covering her hands up to her upper arms. Then she bent over and unbuttoned her black hemline, showing glimpses of her thighs. His eyes widened when she raised her right leg and laid her boot on the table.

Tony swallowed. He scanned her body top to bottom. Nice chassis; he wouldn't mind taking her for a ride.

Lora took out a worn plastic smart card from her upper tights. "This is the deed to my farm. It's worth more than your gold."

There was a mumble around the table.

Hell yeah, this babe sure knows how to deliver.

"I'm calling." Lora fixed her dress and sank back to her seat. "Show me what you've got, sweetheart."

Tony nodded and laid his cards on the table. Daydreaming about winning and telling his boss that he could finally repay his debt to him. He felt like a billion dollars.

"*Read'em* and weep." Lora chuckled and showed her hand.

The world spun around him; he had to grab the table. He took a deep breath and forced himself to stare at her cards again. The black widow had a straight flush. *She just skinned me alive. If I don't want to die, I must do something, quick.*

"Better luck next time." Lora smiled and reached for the ante. She stared straight at his eyes, "Will you be willing to hear my business proposition now?"

"I don't think so." Tony drew his heater. "I'm afraid I can't let you get away with this load, Miss."

Everyone froze; all conversations died, as if an electric shock just zapped every attendee.

She stared at the pistol, then she looked at him with her big brown eyes. "Baby, you have to face reality. I won it fair and square. But as I said earlier, I can offer you..."

"Think you can outsmart me, eh?" Tony raised his pistol and aimed it right between her eyes.

Something bit his neck. He touched it with his free hand and pulled out a tiny white dart.

"I'm sorry it had to come to this." Lora's voice sounded like an echo. "If you want your money back and want to hear about my proposal, you know where to find me."

Tony's gun sank to the floor. He felt a sudden dizziness. "How did you..."

He fell softly on the Zeppelin's hard and cold metal floor. The last notion he had before he lost consciousness was cursing the day his parents chose to settle on this God-forsaken moon.

Tony woke up. The first thing he was aware of was the taste of his own blood. His head was tipped back, spinning. He nodded forward and succeeded in closing his mouth but almost fell onward out of the chair. Gripping his head with one hand, and an armrest with the other, Tony opened one eye and saw his boss, Nicholas Dupuis, holding a knuckle duster stained with blood.

"Where's my gold?" Nicholas, known by his nickname Double-Barrel Nicky, spoke in his thick French accent. His voice sounded like a death knell; icicles formed in his eyes.

Cold sweat trickled down Tony's forehead. No doubt, these were his last moments alive. As a runner who lost the Legion's money, a month worth of protection fees from the miners' colonies, he had no excuse. He spat blood to clear his mouth. "Please, boss, it wasn't my fault. It was stolen from me."

"Don't bullshit me." Double-Barrel Nicky swung his knuckle duster and smacked Tony on the head. "*Merde*, after all I'd done for you, at least be honest enough to tell me the truth. *Oui?*"

The pain was unbearable. Tony wished he had lost consciousness. He felt tears forming in his uninjured eye. "I swear; that broad drugged me; she took your swag."

"Do you think I'm an idiot?" Double-Barrel wiped the blood stain off his pressure suit. "A broad, you say?"

"Lora Morel. The farm girl."

"Lora?" Double-Barrel burst into rolling laughter. "That *demoiselle* pulled the sting on you?" It took him a long moment to calm down. "I'll tell you what..."

Tony's saw a shred of hope as his boss' mood shifted.

"I know where her farm is." Double-Barrel's voice became serious once again. He took his helmet which was laid on the table. "Waste her, and get my gold back. Then I might, just might, forgive you."

The Legion tolerated no failures. Under these circumstances, Tony expected his boss to put a bullet through his head, no questions asked. But Nicky had a soft spot in his heart.

"I'll do her for you, boss," said Tony. "Trust me, I will."

Double-Barrel handed Tony a handkerchief. "Clean yourself, boy. You look like shit. Get some sleep. Tomorrow, we'll pay Lora a visit."

###

Escape Velocity

Sneaking up on someone in broad daylight was sheer stupidity; especially when she lived on an isolated airborne farm where any approaching airship could be seen from miles. Unfortunately, Tony had no choice.

Double-Barrel Nicky maneuvered his small two-seated Zeppelin toward the farm's docking bay.

The airlock reminded Tony of a conversation he once had with an old NASA engineer. He remembered him saying how lucky they were that Titan had a thick atmosphere. It had something to do with having the same pressure inside and outside, which made airlocks really simple, at least in the old man's mind.

"Don't show your face, unless you pop her." Double-Barrel Nicky smiled as he made his infamous cutthroat gesture, leaving no room for imagination regarding what would be Tony's fate if he failed to complete his mission.

Tony contemplated what was scarier, to face the smart-ass farm-girl that wiped him clean or to turn back and face Double-Barrel. He gripped his assault rifle firmly, and stepped into the greenhouse.

The scent of fresh vegetation filled his lungs, so different from the smell of the filtered air he was used to.

A shadow moved behind the green bushes. Tony raised his gun and released a short burst. The recoil pushed him backward, and he almost lost his balance. Shootings had to be handled real gently in Titan's low gravity.

He heard a scream, and the figure dropped. Tony walked toward the motionless body. The corpse was wearing a brown jacket stained with blood; its skull, which was covered by remnants of an aviator hat, was smashed by the direct headshot.

Tony had mixed feelings. He had to kill Lora. His life and his honor depended on her being dead. On the other hand, she was a cute darling, a charming lady he would hate to waste. He sighed as he turned the corpse with his rifle's butt.

It wasn't her; his heart raced. It was a body of a man.

"Put your gun down, sweetheart!" A chilling feminine voice whispered behind his back. "Or I'll blow your brains out."

Gee, I admire this girl. Tony let go of his gun and raised his hands. He wondered if he should shout and warn Double-Barrel Nicky. He slowly turned and found himself staring into the barrel of a shotgun. He heard her click the safety off.

"You killed Harry." Lora's voice was as cold as methane ice. "Back on the Zeppelin I told you I'll give you your damn money back." She spat on the floor. "You should have listened to my business proposal. Goddammit, I need the help of your Legion. But, no," she sighed. "You had to burst in with blazing guns like a rabies infected mad-dog."

"I'm sorry. It was just business."

"I can't say I feel sorry for the scumbag," said Lora, gesturing at the corpse. "But he was a good airman."

Tony swallowed; she had all the reasons in the world to waste him.

"Now where am I gonna find new mercenaries for this job?" She tightened her grip on the shotgun. "Give me one reason why I shouldn't kill you right here and now."

Tony looked straight into her eyes. *Gosh, she is beautiful.* "Because you're not a cold-blooded murderer like me?"

"Wrong answer." Lora said flatly, her expression stiffened. "You surface rats have no idea what I had to do to survive." She raised her shotgun; her finger slowly squeezed the trigger.

Tony's mind raced. In recent years, pirates from the asteroid-belt mining colonies had raided the upper atmosphere settlements. If Lora had survived such a raid, there was no doubt in his mind that she wouldn't hesitate to kill.

"How about filling in for Harry?" He desperately tried to find excuses for her to keep him alive, no matter how lame. He shut his eyes, expecting his brain to be blown away any second.

"Are you a certified aviator?" she asked.

"I'm a fast learner." He opened one eye, and looked at her reaction. "If you let me live -- I promise I'll do whatever you ask me. Trust me."

"Um," said Lora. "There is no way you can step into Harry's shoes." She nervously looked at her wristwatch. "But you're my best chance to enlist the Legion. So, I guess I'll have to settle for you." She waved her shotgun and smiled. "We're going for a little trip, sweetheart. Oh, and by the way, about trusting you -- ain't gonna happen."

She struck his head with her shotgun's butt, and the world turned black.

###

Someone untied Tony's hands and removed his eye cover.

"Holy Maria!" Tony almost chocked when he saw the monster who stood above him. With airplane-sized wings attached to the back of a crude iron suit, it looked like a reincarnation of the devil himself.

"Now you're gonna do exactly what you're told!" Through the iron mask, the fuzzy metallic voice was distorted, but no doubt it belonged to Lora. She held her shotgun with her right hand. "We're going for a short trip to the surface, darling." Without waiting for an answer, she threw a parka coat at him.

"Are you nuts?"

She handed him a heavy battery case and a large air tank attached to a gas mask.

"It's minus 270 Fahrenheit at the surface." Tony made a cross gesture, remembering the warnings given to him by Double-Barrel Nicky when he was drafted to the Legion.

"You should see what it's like in winter," she chuckled.

Without saying a word, Tony wore the suit. He put the mask over his face, and sealed the helmet. It stunk like poor quality homemade rubber. Too bad they didn't have enough of the good-old stuff brought from Earth more than thirty years ago.

"Now screw the wings."

Tony wanted to tell her he ain't no fly boy, but seeing her waving her gun suggested that further protest may not be the best course of action.

Suddenly, the floor opened beneath his legs. *Holy shit.* Tony's blood froze in his veins when he found nothing between him and the surface, more than three hundred miles below.

"Don't worry, dear." Lora's shout overcame the wind. "Just wave your wings like a bird. It's not that difficult at zero point fourteen G."

Tony watched in horror as the ground began to spin. He flipped, and saw Saturn, the sun and the floating farm above, followed by Double-Barrel's Zeppelin. To his dread, the airship and the farm were getting smaller and smaller.

"Come on, wiseguy." Lora jumped after him into the air. "Spread your wings wide."

Tony reminded himself to inhale and exhale. Hearing the air flowing back and forth helped him recover from his initial panic. Each of his wings had a sleeve. He slid in his right arm, grabbed the handle and waved. His body flapped in circles. Then he did the same with his other hand, and managed to stabilize himself in a horizontal position.

Flying was pretty swell, once you got the hang of it. With a little practice, and a little guidance from Lora, he managed to glide, turn and even gain height by waving his hands in the right rhythm.

"Hey, wiseguy." Lora's metallic voice sounded curious. "How long have you been living in New-Chicago?"

Tony stared at her. At that angle, the helmet blocked her eyes, but he did notice she still held her shotgun. Not that he wanted to attack her at 300 miles above ground. "Why," he asked. "What's eating you?"

Lora stretched her wings and flew closer. "Nothing special. We have a few hours to kill before we'll reach the landing site."

"Fair enough," Tony nodded. "I was born in the damn Huygens habitat. The one thing my parents taught me was to take care of number one. They hated the idea of being dumped on Titan. They knew Earth won't be around to help them. And I learned the hard way that they cared nothing about helping me."

Lora flapped her wings until she synchronized her trajectory in a parallel route.

Not that his parents had much choice on the matter, thought Tony. Earth had simply deserted the colonists. No supply ships had visited Titan in more than thirty years. "I had five brothers and sisters," he continued. "When I was seven, after failing a grade two assessment test, the mission director forced my parents to leave me out to die. I don't really blame her with all the air and food constraints in the overpopulated habitat."

As they dived deeper, the brownish color of her suit became gloomier; even the scattered ethane clouds shifted their color to monotone whiskey.

"I was lucky enough to be saved by a group of ore miners. That is, if you consider the life of a child who labored fourteen hours a day, seven days a week, in frozen mines for scraps of air and food, lucky."

"How did you end up in the upper atmosphere?"

If not for his iron suit and parka coat, Tony would have shrugged. "I had some talent for weapons. I learned how to use a gun. When I was sixteen, Double-Barrel Nicky heard about my talent. You see, he was looking for new recruits for his security company. He had me brought to New-Chicago, and he gave me an offer I couldn't refuse."

"Double-Barrel Nicky?" Lora asked. "Are you referring to Nicholas Dupuis? The founder of the Legion?"

"The one and only," Tony replied in a sarcastic voice. Back on old Earth, when desperate people had to run from their past, they joined the French Foreign Legion. Sergeant Nicholas Dupuis was the type of person who had to run from the French Foreign Legion. He and his family fled to Titan in the last ship that arrived from Earth during the early 2060's.

"I'm sorry to hear about how your parents treated you." Lora sounded almost apologetic.

"Don't be," said Tony. "Ain't your fault. One reactor in the whole goddamn moon, is simply not enough."

Lora's big helmet nodded as she flew above Tony to his other side. "That's why my parents, along with other NASA engineers, constructed the upper-atmosphere farms. And it wasn't a simple endeavor. You think it's easy to grow crops so far from the sun? Ha! Let's see how long it would take you to set up all these reflecting mirrors, not to mention the time spent in developing genetically-engineered low-light vegetation."

"You hear no argument from me," Tony said. "Speaking of parents, are yours still around?"

"My father is dead, and my mother was taken." Lora hissed as she glided closer to him. "Twelve years ago. Pirates from the asteroid belt."

Tony couldn't help feeling sorry for the poor girl. Double-Barrel had ordered his men to avoid any contact with the pirates, who had superior weapons and orbital lasers. But he heard stories. He knew that the pirates had pillaged the upper atmosphere settlements for food, electronic equipment, and women. On occasions, they even raided the Huygens habitat

After all she'd gone through, growing up to be a real doll was something to admire. Too bad he had clear orders to kill her. He tried to convince himself that he shouldn't spare any sympathy on the foxy chick. And besides, she cheated him on that card game that almost cost him his life.

They descended for hours. Below, Tony saw a familiar mountain range, perhaps one hundred miles long and twenty miles wide, with summits covered by ice.

As part of the Legion's security business, Tony had flown down to the surface on a number of occasions. He knew the white sheet was a mixture of water ice and methane snow. Although his suit was set to maximum heating, the cold still crept in. He hoped his batteries would last.

"Where are we flying, miss?" Tony finally asked. "You know we can't hide from the Legion." He caught himself using the term 'we'. 'He' wasn't hiding. He was sent to ice her.

Lora flapped her wings. "Do you know how long it was since we lost contact with Earth and the other colonies?"

"Who cares? The damn Terrans deserted us when they abandoned the space program."

"We don't know that happened." Lora made a buzz above Tony's head. "Thirty years is a long time. And since the pirates stripped us of our large radio-telescopes, computers and God knows what else, no one knows what really happened on Earth."

"Well, maybe no one but Double-Barrel. Regardless, I'd never seen a Terran ship in my life." Tony raised his eyebrows. "To me it just looks like Earth deserted us."

"Indeed," Lora turned her head toward him as they flew side by side. In spite of the mask, her metallic voice sounded bitter.

Tony knew how tough the early years were after they've lost contact with Earth. 2,500 colonists strained within a 300,000 square foot habitat—no fun at all. Not to mention the limited Uranium supply for the colony's single reactor.

"I still have nightmares when I think of the disgusting food in the habitat." Tony wanted to puke as he remembered the white mush produced by the reactor at the center of the Huygens habitat—the revolting rations made by fusing Titan's carbohydrates and ice water. "Too bad only the damn pirates were left with spacecrafts."

"Imagine what we could do if we could find one of these spacecrafts." Lora sounded impassioned. "With an armed vessel we might have a chance to fight the pirates. We could fly back to Earth and get more Uranium, seeds and livestock." She flew closer and lowered he voice to a whisper. "What if that spacecraft came equipped with a 3D printer? We could use it to print as many new microchips as we want."

"A spaceship equipped with a 3D printer? Yeah, right. And Santa has wings and he belly dances under Kraken Mare." Tony dismissed the matter.

"Do you remember the day we played cards together?"

"Screw you!" Her comment reminded Tony of his duty to the Legion. If only he could get her rifle.

"A few hours before we met on the Zeppelin," Lora continued, "I intercepted a radio signal from space."

Tony didn't care. His mind was fixed on how she cheated him on the card game. And besides, since the early pirate raids, no one on Titan had a working interplanetary radio. Not even the director. Sure, a few short range walky-talkies remained, and he heard stories about a crazy scientist who had built vacuum-tube short-wave radios. However, he doubted Lora had had access to any of those.

"It was a distress call from a spacecraft orbiting Titan." Lora's metallic voice clicked. She paused for a long moment, as if she'd lost her words. "And it was losing altitude."

"That's bull," said Tony. "No belter ship had ever crashed on Titan. And even if one does, what is it to me? Why should I care if the bastards on board die?"

"Hehehe." Lora giggled. "Trust me, I hope the pirates ran out of air and died a horrible death. Nevertheless, if we can salvage the craft..."

"What were you doing on that Zeppelin?"

"The Legion is the closest thing to an army here. I wanted to draw your attention." Lora laughed. "No hard feelings, I hope." She turned her mask straight at Tony. This time, he could see her eyes through the frosted goggles. "The spacecraft," said Lora, "crashed on this mountain on January 17th." She turned her head toward the ridge below.

"What a nice pirate," Tony sneered. "Very considerate of him to crash just below New-Chicago."

"Maybe the captain figured out he had a better survival chance if he crash-lands near the habitat? Who cares? All I know is that the distress beacon came from the mountain below."

Tony swallowed. The shooting star's image he saw on the Zeppelin on the day he played against Lora popped into his mind. "I'll be damned. You brought me here to help you scavenge the wreck."

"Scavenge? Ha! You're not thinking big enough."

"What do you mean?" ask Tony.

"There!" Lora shouted. She folded her wings, and she slowly dived toward a dark crater west of the northern ridge.

This was the chance Tony was waiting for. He could run away. New-Chicago was too far up. He wasn't sure he had enough oxygen and battery power to fly there. But if he remembered correctly, the Huygens habitat was less than one hundred miles away. Then again, if he ran to the habitat, how could he face Double-Barrel Nicky without carrying out his order? In a split of a second, he made up his mind.

From above, the black spacecraft looked like a house sized saucer. At least, that's what Tony thought in the dim orange lighting. In spite of the impact crater, the spaceship's wreck looked relatively intact. Lora stood in front of the ship, touching it as if searching for something.

Tony waved his wings, circling Lora like a vulture around a dead corpse. As much as he hated the idea of killing Lora, he knew what he must do. Dismissing any other thought, he folded his wings and dived.

They both collapsed from the crashing blow. Tony kicked her metal armor as she rolled on the snow.

"Tony!" Lora screamed; her voice filled with shock and despair. "Don't!"

Her cry broke his heart. He froze for a split second. *No! I must complete my job. What choice do I have?*

Lora lay on the ground and held her rib cage with both her hands. One of her wings broke, and traces of frozen blood spotted the white methane snow.

Her suit must have been ruptured, but the hole couldn't be seen. Her wound must be deep if her bleeding oozed through the thick parka. A small hole wasn't enough to kill a person; Titan's nitrogen atmosphere was too similar to air. The best way to ensure her death was by cutting off her oxygen, or her heating.

The shotgun was attached to the side of her air tank. He grabbed it and aimed at her head at pointblank. Under normal conditions, his glove would have been too bulky to fit a trigger housing, but the trigger on this shotgun had no protection.

Twisting in pain, Lora turned to face him. She looked straight into his eyes; her pupils widened. Tony slowly squeezed the trigger. He felt tears flowing down his cheeks. His heart wept. He shut his eyes when he finally heard the click.

Nothing happened.

He felt a punch in his nuts.

"You idiot!" Lora said. "Gunpowder doesn't work at this temperature."

Her kick didn't do much to his iron suit. Tony dropped the useless gun, caught her with both his arms, and threw her upward.

She tried to spread her wings, but only the non-broken one stretched. She desperately flapped her functional wing, as she slowly spun downward in a spiral route.

Tony waited patiently.

Lora hit the ground, "Tony, don't ..." She tried to stand, but her legs collapsed. "Titan needs you. This ship is Titan's best chance ..."

Tony wrapped his hands around the top of her air tanks, ready to tear the pipes apart.

"Think of the colonists." Her voice was faint. "You can't deny them their only hope for freedom." She pointed at the crashed spacecraft.

Watching the helpless woman wrapped inside the leaking suit made his eyes sting. If they could renew the lost contact with Earth or Mars, if they could re-establish the supply of Uranium, microchips, and seeds... But this pirate spaceship was nothing but a wreck. He wanted to let her live, but not when it came with betraying the Legion. *What good is a good deed, if you're dead?*

He took a deep breath and tightened his grip on her air pipe. The image of this beautiful woman suffocating, or freezing by inhaling the icy air, caused his stomach to revolt. All he had to do was tear off the pipe, yet his hand didn't move. How could he, a loyal *Légioner*, be such a spoon? He wished he had some whiskey with him; not just one bottle, but a whole case.

He sighed; then he slowly turned Lora's air pipe counter clockwise. *Better her than us both.*

Suddenly Tony heard a humming voice from behind, followed by a hiss. He turned his head, and his jaw dropped open.

The noise came from the pirate spacecraft. A man-sized octagonal opening appeared on the saucer's hull. Behind it, he saw a small room flooded with bright light. In it stood a figure wearing a slick white pressure suit, unlike any of the worn-out pressure suits Tony had ever seen in his life.

The figure lifted its right hand and saluted. "My name is Ying Sun. I came from Earth."

Tony stared at Ying Sun suspiciously. Then he remembered Lora. He let go of her air pipe. He released a sigh of relief when he saw her moving. He approached her, "are you okay?" he whispered?

She nodded.

"Earth?" Tony looked once again at the astronaut; he stepped back, and held his head with both hands. "I'll be damned!"

The End.

Crash

Rogue Element, a story combined of Crash and Amber Sky received an Honorable Mention in Writers of the Future contest, 1ᵗʰ quarter 2016

Near Saturn, January 16th, 2097

Ying Sun tapped the rusty control panel. The fuel indicator needle sat near zero. She turned off the *Rolling Stones* music and brought up the *Zheng He*'s schematics on the main display. Her finger slid over the scroll wheel, switching the image to the planned trajectory through Saturn's rings.

"Looking at the fuel indicator for the thousandth time won't change our propellant level," the voice of Zhulong, the ship's A.I., came through the vessel's speakers. "Forget it, missy. We don't have enough fuel to attempt an alternate maneuver. Your time would better be spent preparing the landing gear or fixing the leak in compartment C24." Zhulong's snakelike image appeared on the monitor. "We don't want another engine failure now, do we?" He grinned.

"Shut up, Zhulong! You're pretty annoying for a computer." She wished the spacecraft had a simple autopilot nav system, and an off button for this irritating Artificial Intelligence. But it wasn't like she had a choice in this matter. As the only survivor of the People's Liberation Army Inner Mongolia detachment, she was lucky to find this piece of junk vessel in an abandoned test facility. All things considered, being alone in space with an irksome virtual talking dragon was far better than being hunted down by brainwashed gamers in the scorching Gobi Desert.

"You're one to talk," a smirking Zhulong retorted and faded, leaving Ying staring at her own reflection.

She looked older than her thirty-year-old self. Dark circles surrounded her eyes and, in the zero-gravity environment, her unwashed hair was a mess. "Motherless goat of all motherless goats," she yelled and kicked the base of the panel. Being reminded of the grime and sweat of two weeks without a shower made her itch.

###

Ying looked through the window as the *Zheng He* got closer to the gas giant's rings. Saturn grew bigger. She drifted to the command chair and buckled in. The *Zheng He* was a thirty-year-old warship, a relic of the Chinese Space Force. With all the leaks, corrosion, broken systems and shortages of air, water, propellant and ... well, of just about everything, she had to wear her EVA suit at all times. Ying ignored the helmet beside her. She didn't want to put it on; her own body odor was just too strong.

The *Zheng He* was now close enough in its approach that Ying could see the rings' meteoroids. Most of them were smaller than a tennis ball, but some were as big as a house. She felt an urge to bite her fingernails, if not for her gloves.

A wail of alarm and the beeps of priority signals broke the silence.

"Proximity alert!" Zhulong announced.

"Oh shit, oh shit, oh shit!" Ying gripped her seat tight. She stared out the front window with her eyes wide open. It didn't matter how many times Zhulong had told her that the gap between the F and G rings was statistically safe, she still hated the idea of passing through it. The fact that the *Cassini-Huygens* spacecraft had plunged through the gap more than ninety years ago with no issues didn't mean squat. *Cassini-Huygens* had been a tiny, unmanned vessel, unlike the two-thousand-ton Chinese space cruiser she was in. Ying hoped her ship had sufficient fuel to attempt a safer slowing maneuver.

The external cameras displayed little puffs of plasma, as thousands of dust particles collided with her ship at twenty kilometers per second.

She held her breath, wondering how many meteoroids sped pass the spacecraft's bow.

A few seconds passed, and the *Zheng He* cleared the ring.

Ying threw her hands in the air. "We've made it, Zhulong. I shouldn't have doubted you." She wished he was flesh and blood so she could hug and kiss the annoying A.I.

BANG! The side panel blew up. Debris flew through the air in a dangerous shower of sparks. A fireball engulfed the bridge. The walls, the control panel, and her own chair burst into an inferno.

Ying screamed in agony. The flames consumed everything in their path. Her EVA suit blocked most of the heat, but she wasn't wearing her helmet. She covered her eyes, trying to stay conscious amid the firestorm. But the pain ... "Ahhh!" She could smell her own skin burning.

A cold spatting of liquid covered her blisters as a hiss filled the bridge. She thanked her ancestors and the Three Star Gods that the fire suppression mechanism was one of the few systems that remained operational.

"What's wrong? Are we hit? Did we lose the engine?" The words coming out of her mouth sounded weird, as if she'd had her entire mouth numbed at the dentist. With all the smoke and the steam, she couldn't see the monitor. She untied herself and searched for the first-aid kit.

"Zhulong?" The A.I didn't respond. The monitor, covered in melted aluminum, was dead.

"Please, please, please. Not now." Ying frantically checked for loose cables. She mashed the power button. Nothing.

The low pressure alarm howled. There was no time to diagnose Zhulong or worry about personal first-aid. "Sorry, friend." Ying grabbed her helmet and put it on.

Titan appeared in the front window. Saturn's largest moon was still nearly 1.2 million kilometers away. Ying wondered if the Titan colony, her goal, had survived. The colony hadn't responded to her long range transmissions. Would she be able to make contact with the settlers once she was in orbit? She had no fuel, her ship was breaking apart. It's not like she had other alternatives. She adjusted the controls on the mostly undamaged panel and switched on a small microphone.

"Mayday! Mayday!" she shouted in English into the microphone. The pain was unbearable. She struggled not to faint. "Can anyone hear me? Mayday!" She forced herself to speak.

Nothing but static. Not that she had much hope, given that no one had responded to her long range radio calls since she'd fled Earth.

"Mayday! Mayday! This is Ying Sun from the Chinese cruiser *Zheng He*." Ying breathed heavily. "My vessel is damaged and I require immediate assistance."

"I can't hear …" A woman's faint voice came through the speakers. "My name is Lora … from the Titan colo… shortwave … you."

Ying nearly jumped in joy. Someone was alive on Titan.

She tried to re-establish communication. But no additional response came.

She stared out the window as Titan slid across the sky. Her ship was slowly spinning out of control, and her A.I. was dead. She would have to make her approach manually. She pulled out a paper-thin tablet and swiped through the screens until she found the trajectory simulation. At sixteen kilometers per second, it would take her twenty hours to reach Titan.

Ying cleared the ashes off the pressure gauge. Great, zero atmosphere. She sighed. Twenty additional hours with her stinky helmet on and no access to a first aid kit or washroom.

###

Ying was exhausted and so was the ship's fuel. With her and the *Zheng He* both running on vapors. She had managed to crash-land the *Zheng He* on a snow-covered mountain ridge, about a hundred and fifty kilometers from the location of the *Huygens* habitat.

She initiated a self-diagnosis. The results were off the scale. The only bright spot was that she had sustained no bone injuries and only superficial damage to her EVA suit. She released a sigh of relief and made a mental note to give a generous offering to her ancestors.

"Zhulong, are you there?" After twenty hours of numbness, she was able to talk with slightly less pain. "If you can hear me, just be aware that we've made it."

No answer came. During her voyage from Earth, she'd gotten used to the maddening A.I. But now when it went dead, she realized he was her only friend.

Burnt debris covered the floor and the panels. Ying thought Earth was bad, a place she had desperately fled, but at least it had breathable air. Now, unless she could contact the colony, she'd be marooned on a frozen, unhospitable moon with her virtually dead ship. She unbuckled herself, and tried to walk around. It wasn't anything like weightlessness, but she felt extremely light. It was going to take her time to learn to walk here. For now, she would have to hop around like a slow-motion kangaroo.

Her EVA suit stank of urine, sweat and burnt skin. The facial burns were extremely tender. Since she couldn't remove her helmet to inspect the damage, she decided to check on Zhulong.

The lights went off.

"Really?" Ying slapped her hip, questioning the wisdom of the universe. "Now the batteries are dead? What have I done to deserve this? Did I offend someone?"

Ying turned on a small, helmet-mounted flashlight. She jumped to the control panel, opened a hatch and typed.

"Speak to me, buddy. For the last two weeks I could never get you to shut up. Now, that I need you, you decide to go quiet?" She punched Zhulong's monitor in frustration, stirring aluminum dust. The monitor remained offline.

"I'm going to die, alone." Tears flowed down her burnt cheeks.

"Get a hold of yourself, Ying," she spoke aloud. "You're the commander of this damn ship. Now calm down! That's an order!" She slowly sank to the floor. "I know where I am. I'm not too far from the *Huygens* habitat. Even exhausted, I should be able to cover the distance in a few hours. Also, before I crashed I spoke with someone on the radio. As far as I know, a rescue mission is on its way. Now, Ying Sun, what's next on the agenda?"

She looked around the devastated bridge. "Radio. I must power the radio."

A few more clicks, and she manually kick-started the backup generator. Bright light flooded the bridge. Now she was able to see the full extent of the damage. The radio and the microphone had been smashed. A giant metal plate that fell from the ceiling had shattered it. Ying stared at the crushed radio with her mouth wide open.

The terrain was covered with a thick layer of methane snow, which Ying managed to walk on without sinking in. Thank the gods for Titan's low gravity. When she reached the summit, she turned and stared down at the *Zheng He*. Her ship rested on the side of the mountain, perhaps five hundred meters below her.

"Poor girl." Ying said to her spacecraft, as if the ship could hear her. "You're not going to fly anytime soon." Her mind lingered on the virtual dragon, the dead heart and soul of the old ship.

To the north, Ying could see a dark methane lake. To her east, a second mountain ridge blocked her view. She stared at the ridge for a long moment.

"Hello." She shouted, ignoring the pain. "Can anyone hear me?"

Nothing but the echo in her helmet and the howling wind.

"Figures." She shrugged.

Ying kneeled and took out her folded tablet from a pouch attached to her leg. With Zhulong's breakdown, this device was the only Titan map at her disposal. She unfolded the paper-thin tablet, laid it on her hip, and moved her gloved finger along the center until she found the location of the *Huygens* habitat. Ying stood and flipped the tablet, holding it upside down, examining the lake and the ridge. She shook her head and sighed. The distance was way too far.

Suddenly, a strong gust snapped the lightweight tablet out of her hands. The flexible material fluttered and flew into the air.

"No, no, no, no!" Ying cried in panic.

She jumped and missed the tablet by a centimeter. She fell down on the slope, leaving a mark in the snow. The tablet flew up and away at an increasing speed.

"No, no, no. Don't!"

A few seconds later, the tablet disappeared into one of the whiskey colored clouds.

Ying fell to her knees and cried.

The *Zheng He*'s external door opened. With her EVA suit covered by a thick layer of snow, Ying dragged herself through the airlock.

She walked to the command panel, turned the media server on and cranked up the speakers. Rolling Stones music flooded the bridge.

She stared at the shattered radio, and kicked it. Then she sat on the icy floor as she burst into laughter. She saluted the dead monitor. "If I could take my helmet off, I would have a drink in your honor, my friend. See you in the realm of the dead … soon."

The howling wind lashed against the metal hull.

"Zhulong, how much time do you think I have before I run out of water, air, heat or whatever? How long before I die?"

No reply came.

"Screw you, Zhulong. Stay dead. See if I care."

Ying crawled on all four to the communication panel. She looked over the smashed radio.

She made herself stand, opened a drawer and pulled out an obsolete paper binder that read 'Ship Schematics'. She flipped the pages until she reached the radio diagram. The comparison to the broken radio was not promising.

"Where in the middle of Titan can I find multi-zpx negators? Dammit."

She continued to flip through the pages. "Not even a walkie-talkie? What a piece of shit spacecraft."

She threw the binder in frustration. It exploded and the papers scattered across the floor. One page settled near her feet. She picked it up and read through the schematics.

She laughed. "The emergency beacon. Yes!"

Adrenaline revived her exhausted body. With new strength, she hopped to the engine room.

###

The five hours that had passed since Ying activated the beacon were the longest period she'd ever experienced.

She heard banging on the external pressure hull. Someone, or something, was outside.

She opened the airlock and found two figures in crude iron EVA suits attached to massive looking wings. One of the figures was standing, tinkering with the backpack of the other, which was on its knees. They both turned and stared at her.

Ying was confused and, in the absence of any known protocol, she decided to salute. "My name is Ying Sun," she spoke English, remembering that the habitat had been a NASA project. "I've come from Earth."

"Earth?" the standing iron-clad astronaut said in a masculine voice. He let go of the other figure, folded his wings and stepped forward. "I'll be damned. After thirty years? We lost all hope of ever seeing a Terran ship again. How is it possible?"

"You must help me." Ying pointed desperately to the inside of her vessel. "My partner … um … an A.I system, is dead. I need a technician."

The kneeling figure raised its head. "Ying?" She exhaled. "Did you say Ying Sun?"

Ying looked to the figure, her eyes wide open.

"I'm Lora Morel." The kneeling astronaut stood up, leaning on her comrade. "I spoke with you on the radio." She paused and took a deep breath. "We came as soon as I detected your distress beacon. We are all safe now." She stared at her male partner for a long moment. "Right, wiseguy?"

"You betcha!" The guy pointed at the *Zheng He*.

Then he turned to Ying. "Let's take your A.I. friend's module to the habitat. I'm sure we can find someone who is able to fix it. That is, if we can find compatible parts."

Through their helmet visors, Ying could see that Lora was smiling. In spite of her aching burns, she smiled back.

The End

Ron S. Friedman

Torn

Honorable Mention in Writers of the Future contest, 2nd quarter 2016

Ceres mining colony, Asteroid Belt, July, 2097

No. For the kids' sake, I ain't gonna do it.

Sabine stared at the sharp kitchen knife in her shaky hand. Twelve long years had passed since she had been kidnapped from her family and given to Isaac Cain as a trophy wife. Twelve years since the last time she had seen her fourteen-year-old daughter. Since then, not a day had passed without thoughts of taking her own life crossing her mind.

"And how's my lovely wife today?" Cain smiled. He leaped forward and landed gracefully next to Sabine. Cain was an expert in controlling his body movement in Ceres' low gravity, which was about one seventh of the gravity on Sabine's home moon - Titan.

"I love you more than anything in the solar system." Cain kissed her on the mouth.

He moved his hand along her swollen belly, then he bent over it. "And how's my little bundle of joy?"

Like so many times in the past, Sabine rubbed the knife's handle, feeing its smooth plastic texture. She sighed, laid her knife on the countertop and gave Cain a hug. "I felt her kicking. I have a hunch she'll be as strong as her father." She forced herself to smile. "Let me give Charlie and Ben a goodnight kiss. Then I'll join you for dinner."

"You have no idea how glad I am we salvaged that fertility A.I. med-kit." Cain blew a kiss.

Sabine smiled. At the age of forty-eight, pregnancy could be a high risk. She didn't want to have more children. Especially not Cain's. But her husband was so persistent he burnt a full year's mining revenue on the irreplaceable A.I. Doctor.

"I cooked something special for you, my love." He pointed at the empty plates laid on the table.

"What is it?" Sabine poked him. She took a deep breath. Something smelled different in the air. Could it be fresh fruit? Here? On Ceres? She immediately dismissed the idea.

"It's a surprise," he chuckled. "For you, love."

She heard a knock on the door, then a hiss. Sami, one of Cain's shipmates, rushed into their unit, breathing heavily.

"Captain." Sami stood in front of Cain, and saluted. "We detected a vessel entering orbit. From the engine's signature, we think it's an Earthen spacecraft."

For a long moment, no one spoke. The Asteroid Belt Mining Syndicate had lost contact with Earth more than thirty years ago. Since *The Catastrophe*, Earth was under quarantine. No one was allowed to land there, and no one was allowed to leave. No radio signals and definitely no spaceships. For all she knew, outside the asteroid belt humans survived only on Mars and Titan.

"Earth? Are you sure?" Cain stared at his comrade. "I'll be damned!"

Cain turned and grabbed Sabine with both hands. "I'm sorry, my love. I must go now. Promise me. Whatever happens, protect our kids."

Sabine nodded.

Cain kissed her goodbye.

###

Charlie fell asleep immediately after Sabine kissed him goodnight. The five-year-old child was exhausted after his two-hour mandatory G-force gymnasium practice. Ben, three years older than his brother, wanted her to read him a bed-time story.

Sabine took a tablet from the shelf. An archaic electronic device Cain looted during last year's raid on Titan's colony. She sat on the lower bunk bed, next to Ben, who was already inside his little attached sleeping bag. She read for him a story about two kids, a brother and a sister, who were lost in a wondrous high gravity green place called a forest.

When Sabine finished, she gave Ben a kiss on his forehead. Before turning off the lights, she glanced once more at her lovely kids and at the jolly wallpaper that showed polar bears dancing with penguins. When Ben had picked this decoration, he had told her these animals would be a good fit for an icy dwarf planet. He was so cute.

BOOM! An explosion rocked their underground room. She felt a vibration throughout her body. She grabbed her belly, reflexively.

"Mommy, what is it?" Ben asked.

Sabine hugged him tightly. Her eyes darted toward the hatch door.

Then she heard other noises. They sounded like gunshots. It wasn't anything like the rail-guns and lasers which were used by her husband's crew during their pirate raids. These were old fashioned chemical gunshots. Gunpowder, bullets, like in an old movie.

The emergency siren began to whine.

"Mommy!" Charlie woke up. He jumped out of his bed and climbed down to hug her. "I'm scared." He gripped her shoulders and held them tight.

Sabine caressed Charlie's head. "Let me talk to your brother. Okay, sweetie?"

Charlie nodded. He slid into Ben's sleeping bag, and covered his head.

"Listen to what I tell you, son." Sabine took Ben's hands. "Listen carefully to every word. Do you hear me?"

Tears were flowing down Ben's face. He didn't respond.

"This is an intruder alert. Bad people have come to Ceres. But don't worry, son. We'll be safe. Daddy gave me a protocol for this scenario." She tried to inspire confidence in her kids, but her voice was quivering. The last time she had heard an intruder alert was twelve years ago, on Titan, when she had told her daughter to hide from Cain's pirates. Now it was her younger kids' turn to hide.

If she would seal the hatch without extra oxygen, the air would only last for a few hours. It could be worse. The wall could be breached, turning the entire colony into vacuum. "I must go to the main compartment to bring us EVA suits."

"And leave me and Charlie alone?" Ben's face was as white as Occator crater's bright spots.

"I'm going to lock the door behind me. I should be back in five minutes. I want you to stay quiet here. Protect your brother. Don't make any noise, don't come out, and don't open the hatch no matter what you hear. If I'm not back, wait until it's difficult to breathe. Only then open the door, take Charlie with you and go to Aunty Tatiana."

She rocked Ben's shoulders with both her hands. "Do you understand?"

Ben nodded, his wide eyes staring at her in fear.

"What will you do?" she asked. "Tell me."

"Stay in the room," Ben whispered. "And if the air stinks, go to Aunty Tatiana."

"And take your little brother." She hugged him again and she left the room, sealing the door behind her.

More shouting came from the tunnel outside their compartment, followed by screams. Her heart was pounding fast.

Ever since the solar system colonies had lost contact with Earth, the Asteroid Belt Syndicate had been raiding other colonies. It had been assumed that only the Syndicate had working spacecraft. Evidently, that assumption was wrong. For the first time in history someone was raiding an asteroid belt settlement.

In one big jump, Sabine reached the storage room. She pulled out her EVA suit and put it on, as was mandated by the Syndicate's safety regulations. She had to readjust its core to fit her big belly. Then she grabbed the two little pressure suits for her children.

She needed a weapon. She would not be captured without a fight. Not this time. Cain didn't keep any laser-guns in the house. She desperately scanned their living unit. She never had the need nor the desire to use one. Except for... She snatched the kitchen knife and put it in her utility pouch above her gloves.

Still holding her helmet in her left hand and the two kid suits in her right, she carefully peeked through the door that led to the underground corridor.

From a distance of perhaps fifteen meters, Sabine saw Cain and Sami on their knees, hands over their heads. Four people encircled the two pirates. All four wore the same type of crude iron EVA suits, the home-made type she used to see on Titan years before she had been kidnapped.

Behind them, Sabine saw a couple of mining carts filled with computer parts and other electronics, probably collected from the residential units between here and the spaceport.

One of the intruders, a rugged old fellow, perhaps sixty years old, carried a double-barreled shotgun. The other three were a girl in her mid-twenties, a guy of a similar age, and a young tall boy who couldn't be older than fifteen.

The old fellow with the shotgun cocked his weapon. He casually aimed it at the back of Sami's head. Then, *boom*! The gunshot almost deafened Sabine. Smoke filled the corridor, and in spite of the distance, the stench of gunpowder nearly caused her to sneeze.

Shit, shit, shit. Sabine covered her mouth to avoid screaming.

As the thick smoke began to disperse, a huge blood stain appeared on Sami's upper body. His motionless corpse slowly sank to the floor.

Now the old fellow pointed his shotgun between Cain's eyes.

Cain didn't beg for his life. He didn't speak at all. He just stared at the barrel.

There was no doubt in her mind that she was about to witness a second cold-blooded execution.

Mixed feelings overwhelmed her. On one hand, Cain was a ruthless pirate. He had killed her brother. His men had killed dozens of people on Titan and took many of the colony's women as sex slaves. For God's sake, Cain himself raped her, repeatedly. But that was twelve years ago. Since then he had changed. After he got to know her, Cain treated her fairly. He took her as his legal wife. He respected her. He fathered her two wonderful boys, Charlie and Ben. They were the most important things in her life. She was expected to become the mother to his third child, a girl. But could she ever forgive him for his horrendous crimes? *No*, she told herself. She would let these intruders execute the scum. Isaac Cain, a pirate captain serving the Asteroid Belt Syndicate, had no place in this universe. Even though she had never seen a living dog, Cain deserved to be killed like one.

The old man with the double-barrel shotgun slowly squeezed the trigger.

"No!" Sabine cried, surprising herself. She dropped the kid suits and her helmet. Exploiting Ceres' low gravity, she jumped and landed on top of the old fellow.

"*Merde!*" the fellow shouted in a thick French accent. "Do you want me to kill you too?"

"Don't kill him." Sabine begged. "He is a good father."

The old fellow caught her arm and threw her to the floor. She looked up. He aimed his shotgun at her.

"Mother?" said the young woman who stood next to the old fellow. "Mother? Is that you?" She pushed the shotgun aside and stared at Sabine through the transparent extravehicular visor of her helmet.

It took time for Sabine to realize what was going on.

The old fellow lowered his gun and looked at the young woman. "What did you say?"

The young woman slowly took off her helmet.

Sabine examined her. She was tall, as was expected from space-born. There was something familiar about the woman's face. Her nose. Her lips, her facial structure and even her curly black hair … Could she be Lora? Her fourteen-year-old Lora whom she had left hiding on Titan twelve years ago?

"Lora?" Sabine whispered. The words barely left her mouth. She came closer and touched the girl's pale face.

Lora burst into tears. She stepped forward and hugged Sabine. "Mother, this is insane. I can't believe I found you!"

Sabine almost choked. She couldn't say a word. Tears flooded her eyes and obscured her vision.

"Ladies," the double-barrel fellow said, "I don't want to break up this reunion, but we have to move out. Three Belter spacecrafts are heading toward Ceres. They should be here in less than forty minutes."

"Nick," Lora said in a choked voice. "This is my Mother, Sabine Morel. She was taken from Titan during the 2085 raid."

"I'll be damned." Nick lowered his shotgun. "I remember that." He raised his gun. "And I remember this scumbag. This *Bâtards* stole five cases of whiskey from me." He hit Cain's head with the butt of his shotgun. "That's for my whiskey!"

Cain rolled on the dusty floor, groaning and grabbing his head.

Sabine stared at Nick. Now she recognized him. Mr. Nicholas Dupuis. The boss. Also known as Double-Barrel Nicky, the head of the Legion, Titan's local criminal organization that used to extract protection money from her parents. What was her daughter doing in their company?

"These are Tony and Paul." Lora introduced the other two space-born guys. "They're both working for Nick."

Tony smiled as he handed Sabine her helmet she had dropped earlier. "What are these?" He held up the kid suits.

Sabine stared at the two tiny suits. *Shit!* She shook her head and looked at Nick and his shotgun. "Nothing. I was repairing them for the neighbors' children from unit 38."

"Miss Morel…" Nick pointed his shotgun once more at Cain's head. "We need to be on our way now. What would you like to do with this scumbag? I say we waste him."

"No!" Sabine shouted. "He's… He is my… he is my…"

"We are taking both him and my Mother with us," said Lora. "And that's final."

Sabine wanted to protest. Of course she wanted to go back to Titan with her daughter. But what about Charlie and Ben? She couldn't leave them here, could she? She stared at Sami's corpse. Could she really risk exposing her children to Nick? *No!* They would be safer with Aunty Tatiana, as far as possible from this cold-blooded murderer. To protect her children, she must keep quiet and avoid raising suspicion.

"Suit yourself; it's your money." Nick shrugged. He tossed his shotgun on his shoulder and started to walk back toward the spaceport. "And besides, you may have a point. This scumbag may be worth something as a hostage." He smiled, and moved his finger across his throat in a cutthroat gesture.

###

A bright light blinded Sabine for a brief second. A small asteroid exploded in front of the spacecraft, spewing debris in all directions.

"Radiation Warning," announced the ship's computer. Alarms and priority signals flooded the bridge. "Proximity Alert!"

Sabine's neck nearly snapped. Her body was squashed against her chair. She gripped the greasy armrests tight. After living for twelve years at two percent of Earth's gravity, her weak bones and muscles were not accustomed to rapid space-battle accelerations and High-G maneuvers. They had no choice on this matter. Nick had argued that the *Zheng He*'s only chance to evade the pursuing crafts was to enter the industrial prospecting sector—a dense artificial asteroid cluster six hundred kilometers from Ceres.

She felt sorry for Cain, Paul and Tony. Evidently this junkyard spaceship wasn't designed for more than four crewmen. Only she, Nick, Lora and the pilot, a Terran woman called Ying, had seats.

Only when the maneuver ended and the ship returned to micro-gravity did Sabine dare to open her eyes. Vast rocks, debris and molten sand flashed across the front window. The intensity made her dizzy.

The ship they were in, the *Zheng He*, as Lora had explained to Sabine, was a rusty old Chinese spacecraft that had crash-landed on Titan. Lora, with the help of Nick's goons, had saved Ying's life and salvaged the ship. Well… if you could call this tin can a ship.

As far as Sabine knew, the *Zheng He* was the only working spacecraft not controlled by the Asteroid Belt Syndicate. And after decades of constant raids by belter pirates, Lora and her buddies from the Legion had decided to pay a visit to the Syndicate stronghold on Ceres, hoping to steal priceless computer components and perhaps acquire some badly-needed uranium for the Titan colony reactor.

"We have a hole in the auxiliary battery array. We're venting acid," announced the ship's computer.

Sabine took a deep breath. The stale air bugged her since she came on-board. But now she smelled ozone, mixed with the stench of burnt rubber.

"Crap! If we can't lose those three pirate vessels," Ying pointed at the radar screen, "our remains will become a permanent part of the asteroid belt scenery."

In front of the *Zheng He*'s trajectory, another nuclear bomb exploded on a small asteroid, releasing a dazzling flash. Like her own emotions, the emptiness of space didn't allow for a blast wave. Mirroring her internal turmoil, the small asteroid began to glow with a yellow-reddish halo. Geysers of melted material erupted. It wasn't long before that asteroid, too, began to break and spread debris into space.

"They are blowing-up asteroids, trying to kill us with fragments," shouted Ying.

"Why don't they just shoot nukes at us?" asked Sabine.

"I don't know." Ying shrugged. "Maybe their industrial-mining devices can't target a maneuvering spacecraft?"

Once more, Sabine heard the thrusters ignite, sending vibrations throughout the ship. Again, she felt the High-G acceleration crushing her pregnant body against her seat. She heard metallic clangs as the hull struggled to maintain contractual coherence. Fortunately, this time the maneuver lasted only seconds.

"Alert! Alert!" the ship's computer announced. A number of indicator lights flashed in red. "I've detected a crack in the xenon tank. And the breach in the solid cooling may damage the integrity of the ion drives." The computer hurled a few more incomprehensible words, which sounded like Mandarin.

Although Sabine had no idea what xenon smelled like, the strong odor of burnt plastic filled her lungs. "What is it saying?" She asked Lora. After she'd finally reunited with her daughter, she would do anything – anything, to protect Lora's life. But she didn't know how. She felt so helpless.

"Beats me." Lora shrugged.

"He's saying that if we won't stop for repairs," Ying brought up the ship's schematics on her display, "the ship will lose interplanetary capacity."

There was a brief moment of silence.

"We'll be stuck in the asteroid belt with only short-range chemical rocket engines," Ying said.

"We're being hailed," said the computer.

Although the *Zheng He* had some military grade machineries, it was an old ship. The white paint on the wall was peeling. Some of the equipment had rusted, and many components were missing, replaced by duct tape and plastic patches.

"Hailed?" Ying appeared surprised.

The computer screen displayed an image of a Chinese gold dragon. "The Syndicate flagship's captain wants to talk to you."

Ying glanced at Lora, and then at Nick.

"Well…" Nick untied himself. He levitated toward the control panel and positioned himself in front of the camera. "Put him on screen. I'm sure we can reach a civilized understanding."

A figure appeared on the monitor. He seemed about fifty years old, a bold character with a tattoo of a skull on his forehead and a black mustache. He wore a black EVA suit decorated with plastic and metal medals commonly seen on Syndicate captains.

Sabine recognized the face. She had seen this captain a couple of years ago at a party. He owned a number of mining vessels and a prosperous sex slave business. She remembered Cain telling her not to speak to him. He had the reputation of being ruthless. She had been told he always got what he wanted, including women owned by other Syndicate captains. There was something about his eyes; some sensation that made her recoil in her seat. She gulped.

"*Bonsoir, Monsieur* Mackintosh," Nick said in his thick French accent. "A personal call. Why do I deserve this honor?"

Mackintosh examined Nick for a long moment. Then he burst into rolling laughter. "Double-Barrel Nicky. And I thought this was an Earthen vessel. I should have known better."

"As you know…" Nick continued, "I'm a busy person. Perhaps we should skip the pleasantries and get down to business."

"Agreed." The monitor showed the serious expression returning to Captain Mackintosh's face. "Well… shall we start by examining the tactical situation?"

"Be my guest," Nick replied.

"We have three ships, you have one." Captain Mackintosh grinned. "Our ships are in optimal condition, yours is damaged, venting gas. Our ships are armed with mining lasers, yours isn't. We have nukes, you don't. We're expecting more reinforcements, you aren't. Tell me, my friend, where the hell did you get this piece of junk?"

"What is it that you propose?" asked Nick.

"Surrender your vessel. And I'll give you my personal guarantee that you shall all live."

"That's so kind of you." Nick's voice turned sarcastic. "But I feel a little too old to start a new career as a beggar in Ceres slums. Perhaps some other time."

"The other option is that I'll give the order to destroy your ship."

Sabine heard whispers between Paul and Tony. Their faces were as white as an ice comet.

"*Monsieur* Mackintosh, my view of the tactical situation is somewhat different." Nick's voice turned serious. "My dear old friend, you know nothing about the configuration of this vessel. Let me enlighten you."

"I'm all ears." Mackintosh settled in his captain's chair.

"The *Zheng He* is a Zhulong class Chinese battle cruiser," Nick said stoically. "Unlike your ships, which were designed to use lasers or nuclear charges against, um, minerals—this *mademoiselle* was designed to battle American, Indian and Russian space fleets. In fact, just before you hailed us I was about to give an order to blow your civilian grade mining vessels into radioactive dust."

Sabine exchanged glances with Lora and Ying. Ying shook her head as if she had no clue what Nick was talking about. Lora shrugged. Sabine scanned the bridge, looking for some kind of weapon controls. She stared at the *Zheng He*'s schematics which were visible on Ying's display, searching for missile silos, energy weapons or canons. She saw none.

"I've played poker far too many times with you," said Captain Mackintosh, "I know when you're bluffing. I call. Show me your hand. Let's see what you've got." He then untied his safety belt and floated above his seat with his hands extended. "Cry havoc and let slip the dogs of war!"

"Wait!" Without fully realizing what she was doing, Sabine jumped in front of the camera. "Wait!"

Captain Mackintosh scanned her top to bottom. His facial expression remained motionless. "You look familiar. Do I know you?"

"Captain Isaac Cain is here," Sabine said desperately. "He is a hostage." She grabbed the camera and pointed it at Cain.

Cain was handcuffed and chained to the airlock's door. He raised his head and glared at the camera.

On the monitor, she saw Mackintosh playing with his mustache. "Well, well…," said Mackintosh, "that's an interesting development. So, Cain, my friend, you've let yourself be captured by a bunch of amateurs? Eh?" He burst into rolling laughter.

"Shit happens." Cain looked back at the monitor. His eye was swollen and he had a few black bruises on his face. "No one, not even you, expected an attack on Ceres."

"True." Captain Mackintosh sank back to his chair. Then he gazed at the camera. "Let's cut to the chase. Nick, what do you want for Isaac Cain?"

"You let us go." Sabine grabbed the camera. She looked at her daughter. She was not going to let her die. Never! "Let us go, and we'll leave Cain behind in an escape pod."

Nick snatched the camera. "And give us five tons of enriched uranium."

"What?" Mackintosh soared out of his chair. His face turned red, and he clamped his hand into a fist. "Five freaking tons?"

Sabine couldn't breathe. Mackintosh tightened his lips as if he was about to explode. In her mind, she saw him giving the order to shoot. She turned her gaze at Nick. She was ready to strangle him with her bare hands. How dare he gamble with her daughter's life?

"Hand over Cain. In return, I'll let you go back to Titan." There was a long pause before Mackintosh continued to talk. "And I'll add one ton of uranium to the deal. One. That's my final position. And I strongly suggest that you accept this overly generous offer."

Sabine looked at Nick. She wanted to scream at him. To shout. To beat some sense into his empty gambler's skull. But she didn't dare to expose their differences in front of the live camera.

"Um... I'm afraid I have to tell you that..." Nick moved his hand along his shotgun. "That we have a deal. One ton of uranium for one slightly damaged Syndicate captain."

Tears formed in Sabine's eyes. She was reunited with her daughter after twelve years of separation, and they both would be allowed to live another day.

"Thank you." Cain nodded toward Sabine after the communication link with Mackintosh died. "Thank you for saving my life earlier, love."

"Love?" Sabine raised her voice. "Love, you say?" She took a deep breath, as if soaking her long overdue freedom. "You think I saved your stinking ass because I love you?" She hesitated. Could she really be in love? But then she remembered her slavery, and her voice once again was full with contempt. "You?" She jumped, landed next to him, and slapped him on his face. Her grease covered hand left a black mark on his cheek.

"I hate you!" she screamed. "You raped me, asshole! You robbed me from my family, from my daughter!" Although he was injured and handcuffed, she kicked him in his ribs with all her strength. Twelve long years of hate and despair were released in one concentrated burst. The kick was so powerful that her body was sent spinning across the bridge.

Cain released a groan. He folded in pain. His face was covered with tears. "But… but… I thought that was behind us. I thought you love me as much as I love you. You told me so yourself so many times."

Sabine regained control. She hovered above the instruments and came closer to Cain. "I was your sex slave, for God's sake. I was forced to marry you. Did you expect me to be honest with you?"

The image of her heartbreaking separation from Lora came to her mind; the rapes that followed; being paraded in chains to the syndicate ship. She could swear she even remembered that during that slave parade, her brother had tried to come to her aid. Nick, his boss, had stopped him, probably to save his life. Nick had even tried to bribe Cain with a case of whiskey, but that didn't help. She had heard from other slaves that her brother had been found dead a few hours later. She blamed Cain.

"Yes, you were taken as a slave. But that was years ago." Cain was sobbing. "You are my wife now. The legit wife I love and care about. The mother of our kids. I'm not the person you knew twelve years ago. I've changed."

Sabine didn't care. She pulled her kitchen knife from her utility pouch.

"Mother!" Lora grabbed Sabine's hand. "We need him alive."

Sabine paused. She stared at Cain, at his bruises, at his chains. She lowered her knife. Lora had a point. She sighed.

###

The indicator above the airlock turned amber and then red. Sabine heard a click when the Syndicate shuttle docked with the *Zheng He*. She heard knocking. A few seconds later the indicator turned green again.

As part of the pact, two of the Syndicate ships had left the sector. The third ship sent a single shuttle, with the intention to deliver the uranium and collect Cain. Simple and to the point.

Nick floated in front of the door, his loaded double-barrel shotgun in his hands. Behind him, between Tony and Paul, Cain was suspended in mid-air, his wrists tied with handcuffs. Both Tony and Paul held a charged heater in their hands. Ying, Sabine and Lora encircled them as the third line of defense. Sabine held a rail to keep herself stationary.

The door hissed open. A breeze cooled Sabine's cheek.

Captain Mackintosh, wearing his heavy iron boots, his black EVA suit, and accompanied by one pirate crewman, entered the *Zheng He*.

"Welcome, *Monsieur* Mackintosh." Nick said calmly, without offering his hand.

Mackintosh looked at the compartment. At the peeling walls, the rusty pipes and the empty sockets. "The mighty Zhulong class Chinese space cruiser, eh?" he said dismissively. "How much do you want for this junk?"

"It's not for sale," said Nick.

"If I thought for a second that your puny boat could pose any threat to the Syndicate," Mackintosh sneered, "I would have blown it to kingdom come, with or without Isaac Cain."

"I missed you too." Nick blew a dust speck off his shotgun. "Speaking of business, where's my uranium?"

"In the shuttle's cargo bay. I hope you die of radiation poisoning."

Nick made a swift gesture with his hand. Paul nodded and rushed into the airlock.

"Glad to see you, Mac." A smile appeared on Cain's tortured face. "Thanks for showing up."

"Don't mention it," said Mackintosh. "I'm sure you would have done the same for me."

A few seconds later, Paul came back, directing a heavy, coffin-sized box into the *Zheng He*.

Nick came to his help. He pointed a small device at the box. Even Sabine could hear the clicks of a Geiger-Counter. Nick laughed. "Titan's mission director is going to pay me a fortune for this shit."

"As much as I enjoy your company," said Mackintosh, "I must apologize. We do have to be on our way."

"So soon? What a shame." Nick, who was busy examining the uranium box, didn't even bother to look at Mackintosh. "Have a safe journey, Mac."

Mackintosh and his crewman turned to the airlock.

"Hey, what's that?" Paul shouted.

Nick raised one eyebrow.

"I think it's a bomb." Paul bent over to look closer. "Standard mining explosives."

"Why you sneaky son of a bitch." Nick cocked his shotgun and aimed it straight at Captain Mackintosh.

Two laser guns appeared in Mackintosh and his man's hands. "Calm down, Nick. Business is business. You can't blame me for trying." Mackintosh and his man slowly retreated backward toward the airlock.

"Give me the disarm code, or I'll blow your head off!" Nick sounded really pissed.

"If you kill me," Mackintosh waved his gun, "you won't have the code. And then, *kaboom*!" He chuckled. "A better strategy would be to give us back the uranium."

"Screw you."

Until today, Sabine had never used violence, not even to protect herself. But this was different. Her daughter was here. She knew Nick. She knew Mackintosh. She knew what was about to happen. She had to act. Sabine slowly floated toward the airlock. Her heart pounded as if it was about to blow, while her hand rummaged through her utility pouch.

Mackintosh's gaze flickered between her and Nick's shotgun.

"My wife is coming with us," Cain informed Mackintosh.

Sabine's brain nearly shut down. She had to draw the last remnant of her free will to force herself not to freeze. She landed softly next to Cain.

"Thank you for saving us." She forced a smiled on her face. She moved casually toward Mackintosh, as if to hug him. Then, she grabbed Mackintosh's head with her left hand, and brought the knife to his throat with her right. "The code, please."

Mackintosh blinked, his laser gun still pointing at Nick. "What the hell are you doing?"

"Look," hissed Sabine, not sure if her knife could pierce Mackintosh's suit. "I had a really *really* rough day today. Trust me. Now if you don't mind, just give me the damn code or I'm gonna kill you right here and now."

Cain smiled, exposing a broken tooth. "You better do what she says."

"I'll be damned." Mackintosh laughed out loud. "Okay, I give up. The code is 'Nick_is_an_ass'."

Sabine pressed her knife against his suit.

"Checked," Paul turned his head. "The code disarmed the bomb."

Nick lowered his shotgun. He scratched the back of his head. "Haha, very funny."

"Now," Sabine said, "I want you to tell your men that you give your personal guarantee to let the *Zheng He* go."

Mackintosh let go of his laser and grabbed Sabine's hand, forcefully moving the knife off his throat. He stared at her for a long moment without blinking. "The *Zheng He* is unique. The only battle cruiser in existence. I decided it shouldn't be destroyed. When the time comes, Nick will sell it to me. For now, I give you my personal guarantee that Nick can safely crawl back to Titan."

He released himself from Sabine's grip. "You need to take better control of your wife, Cain." Mackintosh laughed again as he stepped into the airlock. "She's a real vixen. One that bites."

"Are you coming, dear?" Cain's swollen bruises and missing tooth altered his voice.

Cain's question hit Sabine like a lightning bolt. She had been kidnapped from Titan, for God's sake. She hadn't seen her daughter for twelve years. She'd been a sex slave for asteroid pirates. What was going through Cain's mind? Was he seriously thinking she would give up her chance to restore her old life on Titan and go back with him to Ceres?

"This is my daughter." She hugged Lora. "I love her and I want to be part of her life."

Cain had been a ruthless pirate. But Sabine could see the pain in his eyes. Cain took a deep breath, as if it was hard for him to find the right words. "But I love you. What about us? What about our family?"

"Are you coming?" A shout came from the other side of the airlock. It sounded like Mackintosh didn't have a lot of patience.

Cain lifted his handcuffed hand in a welcoming gesture. "Please come, love." He stared at her. He looked like a lost puppy.

Sabine burst into tears. She would miss her sons, Charlie and Ben. Could she really give up the chance of ever seeing them again? In spite of how she came to Ceres, in recent years Cain had treated her like a real wife. He loved her. But she hadn't chosen to come to Ceres. She belonged on Titan.

She floated helplessly along the compartment's wall, sobbing.

Lora came and hugged her. She moved her hand over her hair, and then she wiped her tears. "I love you, Mother. You know that."

Sabine continued to cry. She was torn between her loved Lora and her love to Charlie and Ben. Why did the universe put her in a situation where she had to choose between her kids?

"You'll not believe how Titan changed in the last twelve years." Lora whispered in her ear. "Do you know we have Zeppelins now? And New-Chicago, it grew up to be a full sized city with nearly seven thousand people. You'll love Titan."

Sabine couldn't stop crying. True, Titan had been her home. Her old home. Lora was her daughter. She didn't want to lose her daughter. Not again. But Lora was all grown up. She was the kind of woman who could take care of herself.

On the other hand, Charlie and Ben were young and defenseless. Was she really selfish enough to dump them and never see them again just so she could go back to her old life? Could she really have her old life back?

"I love you with all my heart." She held Lora's hands with hers. She barely saw her through the curtain of tears. She cleared her throat. "But I have a new family. I'm pregnant, and I have two small boys. Your half-brothers. They need a mother too. They need me. Would it be fair to my unborn daughter to grow up without her father?"

In spite of Mackintosh's shouting, Sabine hugged Lora for a full five minutes.

Sabine took the handcuffs keys from Nick and released Cain. Then, without anyone watching, she collected her knife and inserted it into her pouch. "Come, husband. Let's go home."

Together, they flew into the airlock.

###

"Mommy, mommy, you're home." The moment she opened the door Ben and Charlie rushed to hug her.

"Yes, sweethearts." In spite of her pregnancy, Sabine lifted both of them up. "Mommy is home."

She looked at her apartment and kissed her kids. Then she smiled at Cain. Twelve years ago she was brutally forced to be here. But now her life had changed. Now she knew that living in Ceres was her choice. Hers, and only hers.

"Do you want to see something?" she asked her kids.

"What is it? What is it?"

Sabine let her kids slowly sink to the floor. "Look." She took out a hologram and projected a 3D image of Lora.

"She is beautiful," said Ben. "Who is she?"

"Your older sister," said Sabine in a proud voice. "She lives on Titan. Do you know that she owns a floating farm? A farm that flies high above the clouds?"

"Wow!" said Ben.

"Mommy, mommy," said Charlie. "What are clouds?"

"Mommy, can we go to Titan?" asked Ben. "Can we? Please?"

Sabine hugged them both. "Maybe in the future, sons. Maybe in the future."

The End

Book four: Bonus stories from before the fall

A Matter of Antimatter

First published in *Polar Borealis* magazine, July 2016

"Jeff, I'm afraid we have a problem."

Still wearing his EVA suit, Jeff turned his gaze toward Tim's hologram on top of the control panel. "Now what?"

"I've picked up a fault in the AM25 reactor unit." The A.I's voice sounded stoic. "Expecting an antimatter failure in 55 seconds."

"Holy smoke." Jeff felt drops of cold sweat forming on his forehead. In deep space, this meant he had but 55 seconds before his spacecraft exploded into sub-atomic particles. *No, wait, it's probably 45 seconds now, perhaps even 40.* His mind raced to calculate how much time passed since Tim informed him about the 55-seconds deadline.

Jeff was the only astronaut on board, not counting Tim, the vessel's A.I. unit. There was no point in trying to contact Houston. It would take his radio signal ninety minutes to travel all the way back to Earth, and another ninety for the reply.

"Tim, put the reactor on-screen."

What Jeff saw on the monitor made his heart to skip a beat. The main power cable that fed the reactor dangled in microgravity. Miniature electrical sparks discharged into the air. He took a deep breath.

"Route more power to the confinement field," Jeff ordered. "Use the secondary line."

"I'm afraid I can't do that," the A.I said flatly. "The secondary line is not connected to the grid."

Crap, I'm a goner. Jeff wasted precious seconds trying to focus his mind.

"Open all doors between here and the reactor."

"But that will drain the air," the A.I protested.

"Who cares? I'm wearing a spacesuit. Do it! Do it now!"

"Commencing override to the ship's safety protocols. Doors will be opened in three, two, one..."

Jeff heard the air hissing as the atmospheric pressure dropped. Kicking the wall behind him, he sprang out into the main corridor. No one would ever describe his spacecraft as big, not by a long shot. But when the time given to him was being measured in mere seconds, even thirty feet would seem 'huge'.

He burst into the reactor room. The black AM25 antimatter reactor unit was mounted on the corner rack. The cut off power cable floated in vacuum. But where was the secondary line?

Then Jeff noticed it. *Thank God.*

"How much time do we have before the antimatter confinement field ruptures?"

"About --"

The universe turned black...

The main hatch opened; bright light flooded the hall as a white figure floated into the room.

"You failed the simulation, sonny!" Jeff heard Commander Peterson's voice.

"I failed what?" Jack touched himself in disbelief, verifying that he was still in one piece.

"You didn't think we would send a rookie to Titan in our most expensive spacecraft without proper testing around good old Earth, did you?" the Commander grinned.

"You've got to be kidding me!"

"Mind you, there was a slight technical glitch," added the Commander thoughtfully. "You've awakened in an anti-matter universe. Your original self is dead. Don't worry about it. Happens all the time. Get some rest and we'll re-run the simulation ten hours from now."

"What happens if I screw up again?"

The Commander shrugged. "No idea. Might wake up next to your corpse back in your old universe, or reawaken in this one, or be off to explore yet another. Exciting, don't you think?"

"That wasn't in the contract I signed," Jack protested.

"Contract?" inquired the Commander, evidently puzzled. He frowned. "What's a contract?"

Jack groaned. This multi-universe crap was even worse than he first thought. Bummer. What about his pension?

The end

Ron S. Friedman

Immortality Limited

Honorable Mention in Writers of the Future contest, 4th quarter 2010

UBC, Vancouver, 2032

"Eureka! Look at this, Dama. We made it. I can't believe we finally made it." In spite of the pain in his old joints, Victor lifted his hands and waved the victory sign.

Dama, his young assistant, came running. "Professor, what's wrong?" The lovely East-Indian joined his University research team less than three months ago.

On the lab table, among the Field Emission Display, the 3D holographic terminals, and the multicolored biological computing tubes, lay a simple transparent container no bigger than an ordinary fish tank. In it, a single white mouse ran back and forth.

With his geriatric hearing aid, Victor could hear the mouse's high-pitch squeaks. It sounded like singing chatter.

Dama stared at the mouse for a long moment. "Is that what I think it is?"

"Look how energetic and happy this old fart is." Victor couldn't hide the exhilaration in his voice. He felt like he did many decades ago—hopeful. "Yesterday, this mouse could barely breathe under intensive care. Can you believe this ten-year-old specimen would act like this?"

Victor's heart was pounding as he watched the mouse run. He forced himself to calm down. Even with his new pacemaker, too much excitement could kill someone in his condition. He looked at Dama, at her exotic beauty. She just stood there with her mouth opened.

Mus musculus, the common house mouse, rarely lives for more than three years in a protected environment. Using extreme life extension techniques, including calorie restriction, exercise, special diet and intensive care, Victor's team managed to extend the life of this elderly specimen to the unbelievable old age of ten. That is, if you could call that living.

Seeing this senior mouse running, was like watching a three-hundred-year-old grandpa jumping off his artificial respiration machine, and start jogging.

"My rejuvenation process works!"

All traces of surprise faded from Dama's face. "That means you could win the M-prize!"

Victor could see his own reflection staring at him from one of the lab mirrors. The wrinkles crosshatching his face, the liver spots on his hands and the permanent slump of his shoulders. A pair of bottle-thick glasses perched on the end of his ruddy nose. His bent, skinny, ninety-year-old body seemed lost inside his rumpled lab coat.

"Dama dear," he said softly, "a financial prize is of no importance. Not at my advanced age."

Victor came closer and took Dama's hands. Her skin was so soft and young, it looked so healthy. Despite their age differences he had learned to like her. "Once my process is approved by Health Canada, we'll conduct tests on human subjects. If I can turn back the biological clock on a mouse …" He pointed at the glass tank, and smiled.

No expression was shown on her face.

Victor examined her carefully, trying to read her body language. It seemed impossible for a girl like her to develop feeling for an old guy like him. *Could the equation change if he becomes young?*

"Immortality..." Her voice trailed off.

"Not precisely." Victor shrugged. "People who will go through the process, assuming it proves successful, could still die of accidents, or violence. We will only be immune to age related diseases."

Victor glanced once more at Dama's unwrinkled skin, and then at the mouse. The M-Prize was given by the Methuselah's foundation to any individual or institute that managed to break the age records of a lab mouse.

"According to the readings," He examined one of the monitors attached to the container, "this mouse is biologically eight months old."

There was a brief moment of silence. Dama adjusted her hair, moving a curl behind her ear. She stared at Victor. "How do you think the public may react to this discovery?" She said in a stiff voice.

Victor shrugged. He took off his glasses and started to clean them. His eyes were not as good as they once were. "You don't know what it's like to be hunted by creeping old age. It's once disease after another. It could be cancer, heart failure, stroke, Alzheimer ..." he sighed once more. "As time passes, it only gets worse, the old age monster strengthens while the body's health declines. Until, at some point, the old age monster wins. I can tell you first hand, sick old geriatrics will be thrilled."

There was no doubt in his mind. No doubt at all. People, even young ones, will embrace the cure for humanity's deadliest disease.

"Professor," said Dama, breaking his line of thought as her warm brown eyes crossed his. "Have you ever wondered why no one before today discovered how to rejuvenate people?"

The ability to reverse aging was his lifetime journey. Years after the completion of the human genome mapping in 2003, and the introduction of DNA computers, he discovered how to reverse damage done by Nuclear Mutations. Programmable nanobots systematically scanned random cells and fixed damaged nuclei using RAN interfaces.

But whenever he found a solution to one biological challenge, a new one came along. Aging agents such as Cell Loss, Mitochondria Mutations, Intercellular and Extracellular junk, and Tissue stiffening—all had to be dealt with.

Victor took a handkerchief, and moved it across his forehead. "No one discovered a similar solution because it's a complex process, my dear."

Nevertheless, doubt crawled into his mind. The knowledge and the tools were available for at least a decade. And Mega-Corporations had better resources than what was available to a Canadian university lab. Much better.

The holo-phone rang, cutting his train of thought.

###

The traffic from the University of British Columbia to downtown Vancouver flowed smoothly. Betsi, Victor's Ultracapacitor self-driven vehicle, cruised silently through the streets. Victor remembered the days when people used to drive to work, using smelly gasoline cars. Today, most people worked from home using remote virtual reality offices. Some businesses though, including their destination, TeraInt Limited., kept a downtown office as their headquarters.

"You shouldn't have accepted Urik's invitation." Dama said flatly. "He's a ruthless shark."

"Dama, look at me," Victor said in hoarse voice. "Look how old I am. We're talking about Urik Gish, the richest man in town. He can finance my research. He can shorten the legal process by years. Do you think at my advanced age I can afford to wait?"

Dama looked at him; her face was pale.

She must be terrified of Urik. Is she trying to protect me? Does she really care? How could a young, beautiful woman have any feelings for an old fellow like me?

Betsi turned left on Granville Street. They climbed the bridge, crossing above the bay. "Nice looking boats." Dama said mechanically, pointing at the marina below.

"Yeah." Victor remembered that many years ago he used to sail. Not anymore. His license was revoked six years ago, after his first stroke. "Did you know they had to rebuild the marina in 2025?"

Downtown Vancouver looked so different since the city built the transparent nanotube-crystal barrier to hold the water at bay. He watched the waves splashing on the crystalloid walls. Occasionally, he could even see large fish and other marine life. Too bad the underwater visibility was not as good as in tropical waters.

"You're making a mistake." said Dama. "Don't say I didn't warn you."

His intelligent car interrupted their conversation. "We've arrived."

Betsi stopped on Burrard Street, in front of a huge, four-hundred story building. A fifty-meter-long holo sign flashed, "Tera Intelligence Corporation. The future is here today!"

"Leave the nanobot sample in the glove compartment." Dama touched his hands.

"Why?" Victor felt the warmth of her young skin. He wished his blood circulation had been as good as hers. "Urik may want to see it before he buys it."

"Just in case." Dama's voice quivered. "Don't trust him."

Before long, Betsi's speakers hooked into the building communication system. "Professor Victor Cromwell, research assistant Dama Kapoor, welcome to TeraInt Corporation. Our parking server will take control over your car."

Victor's heartbeat accelerated. His dream was about to come true. Government approval, human trials, finance, researches. Dama didn't trust Urik. But what were his options?

"Transferring control to TeraInt parking server. Good luck, Professor," said Betsi.

The dark black gate began to rise, exposing the interior of the Mega-Corporation building. Betsi, now fully under the control of the parking server, slowly rolled in.

###

"Welcome Professor."

The person who greeted them sat on a black leather chair in front of a huge desk. He wore a casual grey and black suit which fit his slick black hair and mustache. The office was simple, when measured in hi-tech gadgets; nevertheless, it was huge and decorated with priceless artworks. It smelled like a trillion dollars.

Victor recognized Urik Gish, the all-powerful CEO of TeraInt Corporation. He wondered why Dama seemed so disturbed.

"Welcome to my humble office, Professor Cromwell."

Victor cleared his throat and coughed three times, another old age routine. He apologized and extended his wrinkled hand. "It's a pleasure to meet you, Mr. Gish."

Urik looked at Victor. "I wanted to be the first to congratulate you on your discovery. Immortality. I'm impressed."

"Nonsense," replied Victor in a dismissive voice. "It's more like renewed youth. People given the treatment could still die."

Urik burst into laughter. "You've discovered the fountain of youth, don't be modest about it."

Victor tried to relax. He had to. He didn't want to drop dead from a heart attack so close to reaching his goals. The most significant obstacle for a fast enrollment of his rejuvenation treatment was the lack of funding. Backing of a big buck Mega-Corporation was essential. Victor smiled. "I'm happy you show interest in my research. It means a lot to me."

"Are you kidding? Of course I'm interested. The quest for eternal youth is as old as history." Urik turned on his 3D monitor. Victor saw lines upon lines of search results. "The tree of life Biblical story, the Sumerian mythology of Gilgamesh. The Greek gods. Even the famous science fiction writer Robert A. Heinlein wrote about eternal youth. Countless examples in all cultures and ages. You succeeded where the greatest heroes of all time failed."

Victor almost collapsed. His old age monster was close to winning. His worn-out body leaned against the desk. "I'm well aware of those ancient legends. What surprises me," Victor remembered his conversation with Dama, "is that a humbled university professor with a low budget was the first who developed a life extending treatment."

"Eh?"

Victor straightened his back, enduring the pain. "Have you heard about Moore's law?"

"About computing power doubling every eighteen months? Exponentially?"

Victor nodded. "Supercomputers were as powerful as the human brain already in 2017. By 2028, the average desktop beat that. Since then, computing power has continued to accelerate."

Urik shrugged.

Victor adjusted his glasses. His ancient eyes itched. Not many people wore glasses these days, not when a simple laser treatment could fix almost any cornea or lens deficiency, assuming they were young. "The capacity of the Artificial Intelligence running the billion-dollar supercomputer right here in this facility is ten thousand times more powerful."

Urik remained calm.

Victor coughed, "The human genome mapping project was completed in 2003."

"And your point is?" Urik asked, almost whispering.

"My point?" Victor paused for a few seconds regaining his breath. "This technology should have been available in 2025. There is nothing revolutionary about putting all the components together."

"Hmmm."

"How come the rejuvenation process was first developed in 2032, in an underfunded University lab?"

Urik tapped his fingers on his desk and shook his head. "As a matter of fact, you're not far from the truth."

"I beg your pardon?"

Urik' face turned serious. He spoke in a low voice. "Suppose I tell you rejuvenation already existed in 2024?"

"What? How…" Victor frowned. "How come we… I, never heard about this?"

"Let me asked you another question, Professor. Suppose immortality was available to the masses—what then?"

Victor's facial muscles stiffened, "Every year nearly thirty-seven million people die of age related diseases. More than a billion old people have a poor quality of life. Their families suffer too. Rejuvenation could cure humanity's greatest cause of death and suffering."

Urik rose from his chair to face Victor, "It would be disastrous."

Victor stared at Urik with his eyes wide open. The old age monster in his crumbling body, suddenly gained a champion. He took a step back, picked up his handkerchief and wiped his forehead.

Urik glanced at Dama, then he stared at Victor. "Imagine that from tomorrow morning no one would die."

Why would Urik paint the hopes of staying alive in dark colors?

"Today, eight billion people live on this planet." Urik said. "Do you think the planet can provide enough food and energy to support an infinite number of people? What is the limit? Ten billion? One hundred billion? A trillion?" He paused. "Immortality would be devastating for our planet."

Victor flinched. He looked at his wrinkled hands. He remembered his infected bladder, diabetes, weak body, high blood pressure, cholesterol, worn out teeth, tiredness, immune system… he couldn't even list all his medical issues due to memory loss, another age condition. Even so, he considered himself lucky. Many of his friends were infected with much deadlier monstrosities such as Alzheimer's and cancer. A few were paralyzed. No fate was worse than slowly and painfully dying of an age related disease.

How can Urik deny a cure to the most horrible human condition? One which cost the lives of a hundred thousand people every single day? "You don't know what it's like to be old," Victor's voice was shaking.

"I'm sure you've never experienced social unrest." Urik was now angry. "Every generation got ahead in life by inheriting property when the previous generation passed away. If immortality becomes widespread, what do you think will happen?"

"But, but…" mumbled Victor, "we are more powerful and knowledgeable than ever. We have computing powers beyond anything that we, humans, ever had. These are all solvable problems. If sick people become young and healthy, they can become productive members of society, rather than a burden. Humanity could use the money saved from health care to colonize the solar system. Perhaps even send colony ships to other star systems."

Victor collapsed into his chair. He experienced short-breath. "And," he said in a low, defeated voice, "I don't want to die. I don't have children, I invested so much of my time, and I don't…"

Urik changed his tone. "Sending a few thousand people to space won't make a difference. Immortality would never work. If the process is made available to the public, apocalypse will follow."

From his seat, Victor looked at Urik. "That's not fair," he whispered. "I worked so hard, my body is… is a wreck." The old age monster was winning, like it always did.

"Cheer up Professor; I'll tell you why I called you."

Victor raised his head.

"I offer to buy you out. I'll pay you enough so you will never have to worry about anything."

Victor just continued to stare at Urik. "My body is in ruin. I'll soon be dead. What good is money for a corpse like me?" He looked at Dama. She was young and beautiful. She never experienced old age. Had he been her age, he may have accepted Urik's offer. But, he knew better.

"Please listen," Urik broke the short silence. "I will offer you rejuvenation. You would be able to use the process on yourself. I'll give you a new name, a new identity, a new life, and a young body. All you have to do is to sell me all rights."

Victor turned his head and looked at Urik. An offer to be young, healthy and rich. Anything anyone could have wished for. He imagined Dama and him as a young couple. He opened his mouth when another thought crossed his mind. Could he get rid of his own age monster and watch it consume everyone else?

"What about the rest of humanity?"

Urik shrugged. "The rest of humanity will survive a social, demographic and environmental disaster."

"Old people will continue to die."

Urik nodded, "and by doing so, save our civilization from overpopulation and destruction."

"It's a good offer," Victor blew his nose, "save humanity, live forever, and get a load of cash in the process."

"A win-win scenario," Urik smiled, as if he already had Victor's consent. "You win, I win, humanity wins and planet earth wins. So, do we have a deal?"

"Can I ask you a few questions first?"

"Sure," replied Urik with a grim smile.

"How will you prevent the news from reaching the public? I already called the Methuselah foundation."

Urik took out a form and laid it on the desk, "Have no fear. Your disappearance, along with the fact that no evidence was provided, will ease their suspicion. They'll probably think your message was a hoax."

Victor shook his head and sighed. "But rejuvenation is a wonderful gift to humanity. Will it just be stored to collect dust? Won't you use this discovery on yourself? What about saving a few exceptional individuals such as talented scientists and great artists?"

Urik poured himself a glass of whiskey. The strong smell filled the office. "We will use the formula on rare occasions on a few exceptional individuals, a small number which won't upset the natural balance." He put his glass on the desk and handed a form to Victor. "What do you say, Professor. Do we have a deal?"

"Let me guess, those exceptional individuals will be exceptionally rich people?" Victor said. "You want to save wealthy people and let the rest of humanity die?"

"We'll use it wisely," Urik sounded impatient.

"What about friendly politicians? Will you qualify them to be exceptional human beings?" Victor asked flatly.

"Victor," said Urik, his black eyes flashed frozen flames. "Before you continue in this line of thought, please let me give you a warm piece of advice."

"I'm listening," said Victor without a flicker of emotion.

"Don't push me into a corner. All I want to do is to keep the status quo, just as it has been since 2024. You're smart. Take my offer."

There was a dead silence in the office.

"Since 2024," added Urik, "immortality had been discovered seventeen times in different corners of the world. Why do you think the public never heard about them?"

"You managed to buy them? All of them?" Victor groaned.

Dama came from behind. "Take his offer," she whispered, "please."

"You are an intelligent person, Professor." said Urik, Icicles forming in his eyes.

"What did you do with those who refused to sell?" Victor pressed onward.

The remaining traces of kind expressions vanished from Urik's face, "Be smart, Victor. Think for a moment before rejecting my offer. Think about it. Listen to what I have said, I'm begging you."

"What if I don't sell you the process?"

Urik's lips tightened. "I will ask this for the last time," he whispered in a deadly cold voice. "Will you sign the contract?"

Victor looked straight into the old age monster, which, in this room, was manifested in Urik's black eyes. Victor opened his mouth slowly, "I believe both of us already know the answer to that question."

Urik didn't even blink. He picked up his sunglasses from his colossal, dark desk, and put them on his face. "My offer will stand for twenty-four hours, but only if you'll keep your mouth shut. Go home. Consider the implications. Have a good day, Professor Cromwell."

Victor said nothing. He turned around and started walking toward the office's exit.

Dama stood up besides Victor. Her eyes were red, as if she was crying. It seemed that she was right all along for trying to warn him from going to this meeting.

"Are you coming?" He asked her.

###

"Quickly, get in the car. No time to lose."

Dama nodded quietly. She now had to do what she feared would come.

"Mr. Gish may come after us here." The muscles in his face were as rigid as a mummy's.

Dama wanted to say that this would be stupid of Urik to do so in his own building.

However, she couldn't say that. "You're safe for now, as long as Mr. Gish believes he has a chance to buy you, and as long as you keep your discovery confidential."

"That's great news. That means we might have a chance after all."

"A chance? For what?"

"Once we're outside, I'll broadcast my research on the internet. I don't give a damn about the life of one person. The rejuvenation secret should be available to everyone."

Dama's eyes narrowed. She stood motionless beside the car. That was her cue. Her orders were perfectly clear. There was only one thing left to do. She didn't want to do that. She liked Victor, but she couldn't let him go ahead with his plan. Not now.

"What are you waiting for? Get in the car."

Dama looked back at Victor, "I'm afraid…, I can't let you do that."

"What do you mean?" Victor opened the door. "Do you buy Mr. Gish's arguments? That's bullshit. Urik Gish is making billions by selling his reverse aging process to the rich and powerful. He doesn't care about the rest of humankind. He wants to keep the old age monster alive. It will only help his business." He scratched his scalp. "This is bullshit. Rejuvenation won't destroy our civilization. It will set us free. Free of the greatest evil of all time."

Dama stared quoting. "Genesis, Chapter 3, 22:
Then the LORD God said: See! The man has become like one of us, knowing what is good and what is bad! Therefore, he must not be allowed to put out his hand to take fruit from the tree of life also, and thus eat of it and live forever."

"What is this? Have you become Christian?"

"I just thought it would be appropriate," she said calmly.

"Appropriate for what?"

She looked at the old man. "Perhaps the gods don't want immortality to be part of human life? Maybe there will always be some greater force that will stop people from achieving eternal youth?"

"And you… are you… in service of this… force?"

Dama's heart sank when she saw the expression on Victor's face. "I need to fulfill the commitment," she said, her voice quivered, "I took on myself when accepting this job."

"What job?" Victor nearly collapsed. "Aren't you working for me?" He froze, as if finally realizing; he looked at Dama. "Working for me was just a cover. Your real employer is someone else."

Dama drew a gun, and pointed it at Victor. She felt tears forming in her eyes. She liked the Professor, but her commitment… "I'm sorry Professor, but you leave me… us… no choice."

"I see," he said.

"Urik told you to listen." Her voice sounded bitter. "Urik told you to think. Urik told you to wait 24 hours! But, No. You stupid…" She paused for a moment, trying to control her temper. To act like a professional. "You refused to listen. I'm always astonished how smart people like you can sometimes be so dumb."

Dama took a deep breath and regained her stance. "Why did you have to refuse him? Why? Now look at you, standing here weak, old, defeated, and about to die."

"Don't do it," Victor pleaded in a surprisingly calm voice.

None of her previous victims were so still when facing death. Perhaps Victor was used to staring at death in the face.

"I'm sorry, Professor, I have no choice. I can give you a few more minutes, if you want."

"What if I agree to Gish's terms?" Victor's voice sounded desperate. "What if I'll take his money, will you let me go?"

"I'm afraid it's a little too late for that Victor."

Victor lowered his head. "You can't kill me here. The police will connect Urik to the crime."

"What choice have you left us? You said that the moment you leave the complex you will broadcast by wireless the whole rejuvenation process."

"Dama, don't kill me. It's like killing 100,000 people every day. You'll be old one day too. You know it's wrong."

Dama pulled the trigger. "I'm sorry, Professor. I really am."

No gunshot was heard. Only a faint "vooshhhh" sound.

"Ouch…" cried Victor. "That hurts. What was that?"

"A needle, a needle made of a tiny untraceable icy nerve gas."

"Ouch,"

"You will be dead in an hour, heart failure."

"Oh."

"No trace will remain of the shot."

"Hah."

"Good-bye Victor."

"I think I'm beginning to feel it, maybe I'll wait for death in my Car."

"I'm sorry Victor, I liked you, really."

Victor slowly turned around. He opened Betsi's door. Releasing a sigh, he sank into the front seat. "I, I f e e l…" Then Victor's head fell on the panel.

###

171

Dama entered her home. She felt devastated. This was her worst contract execution, by far. She went to the bath to wash off her messy makeup. She was so exhausted, she felt she could sleep forever.

After she had injected poison to Victor, she drove Betsi north on the Sea-to-Sky, Highway 99.

Dama remembered Betsi complaining about her Ultracapacitor being almost depleted. When Dama ordered it to drive into the Pacific Ocean, Betsi objected. The intelligent car couldn't swim. Betsi knew Victor might die inside her. Eventually, since Victor didn't counter her order, the car had to obey.

It took her four hours to walk all the way to Horseshoe Bay. From there, she took the tube to Vancouver.

Dama sat on the couch for a second, trying to gather strength to undress and crawl into her bed. Did she forget something? Perhaps she would remember what in the morning. She closed her eyes…

Dama opened her eyes. The living room was flooded with light. "Damnit." She had fallen asleep without changing clothes. She smelled like a hobo.

She felt horrible too. She liked Victor, the charming old bastard.

Could she have done anything differently? Her job had been to follow him, and to stop him from achieving success in his rejuvenation research. That was her contract, and that was exactly what she had done.

Dama poured herself a glass of orange juice and sat in front of the HD3D.

The juice glass shattered on the floor. Dama's mouth remained open in astonishment. She could not believe her eyes. Right before her, in a perfect 3D image, stood Victor. And he looked better than ever, as if… younger?

The glove compartment! Dama hit her forehead. How could she forget about the damn nanobot sample?

"Increase volume," she ordered the HD3D.

"...Professor Cromwell, were these the same nanobots as in the research you'd published this morning on the net?" The reporter asked.

"An experimental version I synthesized," the Professor smiled to the hovering camera. "If it was just the heart attack, then I would have been at no risk at all. The nanobots could repair any tissue within my body. But drowning is a different matter. I'm lucky to be alive, thanks to my waterproof car, Betsi."

"What an amazing story." The reporter looked at the camera. "A scientist trapped under the ocean, having a heart attack, saved by advanced experimental nanobots and a self-driving car."

The reporter turned back to Victor. "And then what happened?"

"I defeated the old age monster! You hear me? I defeated you!" Victor stared straight at the camera. "And the world knows about it."

Dama turned off the HD3D. "Well, I'll be damned," she burst into laughter, as if a great burden had been lifted off her chest. She liked the old goat. The lucky bastard made it. He truly made it.

For the first time in her professional career, she was happy she had failed in a mission.

Of course, there would be fallout. Urik would be furious. But Dama was confident she could survive Urik's wrath. She'd followed the contract to the letter. She had done exactly what she had been told. The only detail she would have to forget, yet again ... was the rejuvenation nanobots in the glove compartment.

Oh well, I better call Urik and explain.

The End.

Ron S. Friedman

RON S. FRIEDMAN is a Best Short Fiction finalist in the 2016 Aurora Awards, Canada's premier Science-Fiction and Fantasy awards. Ron's short stories have appeared in Galaxy's Edge, Daily Science Fiction, and in other magazines and anthologies. Ron co-edited two anthologies and he received ten Honorable Mentions in Writers of the Future Contest.

Ron's first novel, TYPHOON TIME, will soon be available.

If you liked ESCAPE VELOCITY season one, please consider leaving a review on **Amazon.com** and **Goodreads**.

Season two is coming soon…

Curious about Ron's writing? Visit his website: https://ronsfriedman.wordpress.com/

Made in the USA
Charleston, SC
11 March 2017